DEATH IN DURANGO

Bounty hunter James Slaughter rides into the Mexican border town of Durango in search of a fortune in silver, secreted by his father, Don Arturo. But Dona Andrea, the haciendado's mistress, wants the treasure for herself. As leader Benito Juarez imposes his iron rule over Mexico, the beautiful former nun Angostina struggles to run her orphanage under harassment from Arsenio Romero, the lecherous jefe politico. Can Slaughter find the loot and rescue Angostina from Romero?

Books by Henry Remington
in the Linford Western Library:

A MAN CALLED SLAUGHTER

HENRY REMINGTON

DEATH IN DURANGO

Complete and Unabridged

LINFORD
Leicester

First published in Great Britain in 2001 by
Robert Hale Limited
London

First Linford Edition
published 2003
by arrangement with
Robert Hale Limited
London

British Library CIP Data

Remington, Henry
  Death in Durango.—Large print ed.—
  Linford western library
  1. Western stories
  2. Large type books
  I. Title
  823.9'14 [F]

ISBN 0–7089–4914–2

Published by
F. A. Thorpe (Publishing)
Anstey, Leicestershire

Set by Words & Graphics Ltd.
Anstey, Leicestershire
Printed and bound in Great Britain by
T. J. International Ltd., Padstow, Cornwall

This book is printed on acid-free paper

1

Slaughter had followed a narrow trail that corkscrewed ever deeper into the mountains until he reined in on a ridge. Dominating the valley below was a big adobe house, a tiled turret on each corner, its high walls glowing bloodily in the rays of the setting sun.

'Looks like this is the place.' He swung lithely down from his black mustang and let it seek what sustenance it could among the thorns and rocks.

He reached into one of his saddle panniers and took out a slim brass telescope. He knelt down, fiddled with the sighting as he put it to his eye until he had a clearly magnified view. *Rancho del Oro*, read an ironwork scroll sign over a big studded outer gateway. 'Looks more like a damn prison.'

There was a little sign of life stirring either inside the house or in the *jacals*, the mud huts that clustered outside one of the walls where the *peons* and *charros* would be housed, but a trickle of smoke was rising into the still air so somebody was cooking supper.

Slaughter caught the gleam of sunlight on rifle barrel and moved his glass across to focus on one of the open towers beneath its dome of tiles. Yes, a man was there on look-out. What could they have so precious in there that deserved constant guard?

Slaughter had crossed the border three days before, heading into high-peaked, tangled country where there was little sign of human habitation. It always made him uneasy to be back in Mexico. To be sure there was scant regard for law and order in the southern states of the USA these days in the wake of the war. But down here the people were so dirt poor a traveller might be killed just for his horse. Unless, of course, they were one of the high and mighty rich like the *haciendado* who had summoned him to this desolate *rancho*.

Who the rancher was, or what he wanted with him, Slaughter had little idea. He had been relaxing in a saloon in El Paso taking a hefty bite out of a bottle of tequila after watching one of his prisoners kick the air — a particularly nasty thief, rapist, cut-throat and sadist who truly deserved to end on the scaffold. Yes, he was washing the dust from his throat and the dirt from his system, making a mental vow to be done with bounty-hunting for good, when some dark-faced Mexican kid had sidled up to him. He had pressed a page of a Bible into his hands, or half a page, torn raggedly down the centre. 'You go *Rancho del Oro. Ranchero* in beeg trouble. He pay you many *pesos* you help heem.'

The boy only paused to give him scant instructions as to how to find the place before starting away. 'Hey,' Slaughter had called. 'How do you know who I am?'

'I see you breeng in bad man.' The

3

boy pointed through the saloon door to where the *vicioso* swung in the breeze, finally at peace with the world. 'Many people heard of you.'

Slaughter had waved the half-page at him. 'What the hell's this for?'

'So he know you and you know heem. He has the matching piece,' the boy had hissed, touching a finger fearfully to his lips. 'My master has many enemies. He trust no one.'

'So, what's his damn name?' But by then the urchin had flitted from the saloon and when Slaughter strolled across to the batwing doors to peer outside, he caught sight of him hurrying away aboard a burro berating its backside with a stick to make it go faster towards the Rio Grande.

All very mysterious. What were they so afraid of? At first Slaughter had crumpled the half-page in his fist and tossed it towards the spittoon, returned to his bottle. Damn them all. He was done with being a hired killer. It gave him bad dreams. Five years since the war and he was still involved in killing. Few of the felons he hunted were brought in alive like the fellow dangling outside. They preferred to die in a blaze of bullets, messily and bloodily, trying to take him with them. He was tired of dicing with death. But, it was not death he was most afraid of, it was what that sort of life was doing to him inside, to his sin-spotted soul. He wanted a more peaceful life. He just needed enough cash to buy a nice piece of land. He aimed to settle down, find himself a pretty little *señorita*, raise a few kids of his own.

'What in *Hades* am I doin' here?' he asked himself. He had picked up the crumpled half-page. Somehow it intrigued him. It rested now in his shirt pocket. Why had the boy hurried off, preferring to risk a lone journey through the mountains than be seen with him? Just what was going on? He sighed as he gathered the mustang's reins and climbed into the saddle, bending the horse around and jogging on down into the valley. 'It's the last time,' he muttered, hoarsely. 'After this I'll finish. That's if it don't finish me.' He was no great believer, but he made the sign of the cross across his face and chest just in case.

* * *

When he reached the foot of the narrow rocky pass he headed across the high plain of rock towards the big mansion, now blackly silhouetted in the dying rays of the sun flushing the distant snow peaks of the Sierra Madre shades of pink and blue. In his mind it was as if he heard again the martial sound of the bugler urging him into battle, or the shrill trumpet of the *paso doble* as a bull goes into the arena. He knew he was taking on a mission that might well end with his death. But, Slaughter had a fatalistic streak. A man could die any minute of any day, either at home of a heart attack, or getting drunk and falling under a wagon, or by a bullet in

6

his back. When the time came, that was it, so why worry unduly? He was aware, of course, that those who lived by the gun died by the gun and, generally, at an early age. Life or death rested, it seemed, on the toss of a silver dollar. Still, he wouldn't have it any other way.

He rode deep in the saddle at an easy lope, his boots in the bentwood stirrups, the rig's leather *tapaderos* protecting his legs as he squinted into the sun's blaze. The marskman up in the tower certainly had the advantage of him. There was little sign of activity. A few ragged children squatted around a fire. A couple of Mexican women sorted through a pile of corn outside one of the *jacals*. An empty corral gave no evidence of ranching business. What the hell, he wondered, went on in this place?

Slaughter was one of those *hombres* who didn't give a rat's ass, as they say, about clothes, as long as they were functional and comfortable. His tattered leather top-coat had seen better days. Jeans, too, holed and faded by the sun, might have earned Levi Strauss a dollar a good few years before and their holes revealed the equally bleached, once red, now pink long johns beneath. His latest acquisition was a wool shirt, corded, not buttoned at the front, open to reveal his strong bronzed chest and muscled neck. His once black boots were almost white from want of polish and cracking at the seams, as were his calf gloves. A thin bandanna was knotted about his throat and a red sweatband around his forehead kept the thick black hair from falling across his face. The only accoutrement he kept in perfect condition was the long-barrelled Texan Schofield revolver that hung just to the left of his loins. He figured that position gave his right fist a faster draw and several men had made the mistake of doubting that, possibly because of his casual air, his looks of some no good saddle bum.

James Slaughter was a mixed-blood

— not by choice — on his grandmother's side. She had been raped by a Comanche warrior when crossing the plains by covered wagon, but had somehow survived, had been rescued by white folk, and had borne Slaughter's mother. The Comanche showed in his face, dark and deeply rutted like carved wood. His green eyes in their slits flickered like a lizard's, summing up the terrain, his chances of life or death.

Although he preferred to think of himself as a white Anglo-Saxon, and had some of the solid, honest, even puritan qualities of his Texan — German forebears, and those who had raised him, the Comanche showed in his guile, his affinity with the wilderness, his stoic contempt for physical suffering whether inflicted on him by other men or by nature, and, above all, in his horsemanship. He rode the mustang with a loose ease almost as if he were part of the animal.

The black horse leaped nervously as a bullet chiselled the ground by his

9

hooves: Slaughter automatically stayed in the saddle, tightening his knees and his grip on the reins as more lead whanged and whined away past his head.

'What the hell?' he shouted as he brought the prancing animal under control. 'What's the matter with you? Ain't you been shot at before?'

Another man might have turned tail and galloped for his life, or jumped to take cover in the rocks. But Slaughter knew that would be in vain. The rifleman in the turret could take him out or pin him down with ease. Another shot cut through the leather of his sleeve. 'Hey!' he roared, raising an arm. 'What you playing at?'

The shooting ceased for a few seconds and Slaughter eased the mustang forward towards the great adobe walls, facing the rifleman without flinching. He guessed he would have been surprised if the guard *hadn't* given him a taste of his shooting prowess.

'Throw up your hands 'less you want

a bullet through your chest,' the man in the turret shouted. 'What you want here?'

Slaughter gave a shrugging gesture as he half-raised his hands. 'I want to speak to the *haciendado!*'

The man in the turret considered this and shouted down to someone below. Slaughter sat his horse and waited. 'Taking their time,' he muttered. The ranch house had obviously been fortified against attack by Apaches for there were ports in its high walls for marksmen to aim through. The *peons* living outside would have herded their families into the courtyard for safety. Beneath the sign *Rancho del Oro*, the solid oak doors were studded with iron bolts. It would be a tough proposition making an assault on this baby, Slaughter thought.

Suddenly a woman appeared on the walkway above the gate, looking down at him, critically. She was middle-aged, very Spanish, her black hair drawn back severely into a bun, her dark face harsh

11

as an eagle's. And she had as fierce a regard in her black eyes as that bird of prey. But this, she saw, was no puny lamb she could pluck or frighten away. Instead it was some leathery gringo sage rat she might be advised to be cautious of.

She held a black mantilla around her head and body and asked, civilly enough, 'What do you want?'

'I just told your boy up there, didn't I? I want to see the boss of this place.'

'What for?'

'What for? 'Cause I'm broke, thass what for. Maybe he needs a *vaquero* for a month or so? Or a man who knows how to use a gun?'

'Why should we want a gunman? Who are you?'

'A soldier of fortune. I've been fighting for your president in his war against Maximilian.'

'That ended a year ago.'

'Yeah, I know. Juarez is in his palace in Mexico City and I've gambled and drunk my cash away in those evil flesh

12

pots called *pulquerias*. I should never have hung around.'

'So, what are you doing here?' the woman asked. 'We are very much off the beaten track.'

'Waal, that might be, but it was the track I was following. I'm heading home, back to the good ole U.S. of A. But, like I said, I need to get me a grubstake. I figured you might need some help. Who are you, anyhow? Where's the owner of this joint?'

'He does not live here any more. He lives in the city. I look after things here. We don't run cattle any more so we don't need your help.'

'Yeah.' The guard from the tower had stepped up beside her. 'You better be on your way, *amigo*.'

'Aw, come on,' Slaughter wheedled. 'Where's your Christian hospitality? The last thang I ate was a damn rattler. Cain't I at least water my horse and fill my canteen? Watcha frightened of? I ain't gonna hurt ya. You let me sleep in the stable I'll be on my way in the mornin'.'

The woman looked doubtful, but nodded to the guard. 'All right, but only for tonight. Let him in, Jaime.'

'Gee, thanks.' Slaughter's face cracked into a falsely jovial grin. 'You need anything, lady, you just ask.'

'What would I need?' The woman's harsh face, too, showed a flicker of amusement. 'What could you do for *me?*'

'Waal . . . all kinda thangs.' His grin widened, lecherously. 'Like splittin' logs, or shiftin' manure in return for a hot meal.'

'Ah,' she nodded, 'that sort of thing.' The gates were unbarred and the lanky guard stepped out, his rifle in his hands. 'OK, *señor*, hand over your revolver and carbine. Just a precaution for tonight, you understand.'

'Sure.' Slaughter handed him the Schofield, its chipped walnut butt forward, and unhooked his Winchester carbine from the saddle holster beneath his thigh. 'What you people so jittery about?'

'There are a lot of *renegados* in these parts, *señor*. We trust nobody.'

'Waal, I guess that makes sense.' Slaughter vaulted lightly from the mustang and led him into the courtyard. 'I guess I'm too much of a trusting sort of guy, myself. That's how they conned my cash outa me.'

He let his horse drink at a stone tank and filled his hat to splash water down over his own head. He shook his hair like a dog. 'Wow! that's great.'

He figured that if he did want to find out what was going on in this building he had to play the amiable, harmless hick. To be bereft of his guns made him feel like a hound with his teeth drawn, but it might lull them into a sense of their own safety. It had become the custom in many Kansan cowtowns he had drifted through for a man to be asked to surrender his guns. It cut down on random killings fuelled by whiskey. Anyway, he still had his big, razor-edged Bowie hanging from his belt.

'Hey!' he beamed, looking around him at the high walls as the gate creaked closed, and up at the narrow, barred windows of the tall, turreted house. 'This sure is some place. What was it, some kinda monastery?'

'No, it has belonged to us for many years. We were allowed to retain it for services to the revolution,' the woman said. 'Anyway, as you know, the church and priests are outlawed in Mexico now.'

'*Viva el presidente*,' Slaughter grinned. 'I wonder how long he'll last?'

'So do many others.' She gave her own thin-lipped half-smile in response to his. 'You had better come inside. There is no need for you to do any chores. The groom will take care of your horse.'

Glancing up, Slaughter thought he caught sight of a movement at one of the narrow windows just below the eastern turret, the face of an old man, who had quickly disappeared, possibly pulled back. Was that why the woman didn't want him hanging around outside?

There were a few *peons* around, probably servants, and he could hear a clatter of cooking pans and shrill chatter coming from a kitchen. There were also three lean and hungry-looking desperadoes leaning casually against one of the walls by a door. They were attired in range clothes and hung with iron and bandoleers of bullets. One was as raggedly villainous and swarthy as any bandit who roamed these hills. Another was sharply attired, silver gilt and conchos embroidering his tight velveteens and big sombrero. The third, an older man, looked more American with a grey-flecked beard, battered Stetson and shotgun chaps.

They assessed Slaughter silently as the lady of the house led him towards a door. The American touched his hat to her but she did not speak, tossing her head, haughtily, and stepping into the deep shade of the *casa*, cooled by its four-feet-thick walls. Slaughter nodded amiably their way and followed her swishing skirt. She led him along a stone corridor to what appeared to be a bath-house adjoining the kitchen.

'Perhaps you would like to join me for dinner?' she suggested, turning to face him, speaking in Spanish. 'You understand? I would like to hear what news there is of events in Mexico City. We are very cut off from things here.'

'Yeah, so you say. *Si*, I can speak the lingo, at least, in my frontier style, enough to get by. So?' — he extended his palms towards two big wooden barrels — 'is this where we're gonna eat?'

'No, of course not. But, I have a very sensitive nose and, quite frankly, you stink worse than your horse. So, you can either bathe and change your clothes and dine with me, or, you can stay as you are and join the other men.'

'Well, I guess that's quite an ultimatum,' he grinned, deep grooves cracking his dark face around his mouth. 'I guess I'll plump for you.'

'Right.' The woman went to the kitchen door and clapped her hands and, as Slaughter sat on a stool, pulled off his boots, revealing sweaty and holey socks, two serving women staggered in with big jugs of steaming *ague caliente* which they poured into one of the tubs.

'*Lavarse, señor?*' one plump one giggled.

'Sure,' Slaughter replied, ripping off his woollen shirt. 'If I can git a bit of privacy in this place.'

'You are surely not shy, are you?' The black snake-eyes of the lady of the house glimmered as she took in his wide, bronzed chest, his high shoulders, his narrow waist, and his rippling biceps. He was not very tall but every muscle was honed to perfection. Her glance flickered down to his bulging horseman's thighs in the tight jeans. 'You can put those aside. We will wash them for you. They will be dry by morning.'

'In the meantime what do I wear?'

'We will find you something more comfortable.'

'Yeah, well maybe I'll just hang on to my wallet,' he said, pulling it from his pocket and tossing it into a corner.

'I thought you said you had spent all your cash?'

'Not all of it. I ain't a complete idiot, am I?'

'I wouldn't know.' She turned away as he ripped open the studs of his jeans and began to ease them down. 'Maria will scrub your back, if you like.' He thought he heard her laugh as she walked out.

'Well, ain't that nice, to strip me nekkid and leave me to the mercy of you two.'

He kicked his clothes away, unfazed by being naked before them. 'Hey, just a minute, I nearly forgot.' He took his shirt from one of them, removed the half-page from the Bible from the pocket, bent down and tucked it into his wallet. 'Now let's git on with it, shall we?' He stepped into the barrel and sank, blissfully, into the hot suds, rubbing his underarms with a chunk of black naphtha soap. 'I sure never thought I was gonna git a warm welcome like this. Hey, go easy with the scrubber, Maria. An' don't you go gropin' for the soap between my legs. The looks that lady was givin' me I might be needin' my energy tonight.'

He glanced at the half-open door and was sure that in its crack he saw the gleam of an eye, that on the far side someone was watching him. He heard the swish of a dress and footsteps retreating down the corridor.

'She's a bit long in the tooth,' he muttered, 'but it might be the only way I'm gonna git any information outa her.' He tightened his eyes as Maria lathered the dust from his hair and tipped a jug of water over him. 'Mebbe she's thinkin' the same thang about me.' He suddenly gave a hawing roar of laughter, which sounded like some distraught mule, as he caught hold of one of Maria's mammoth breasts through her blouse in one hand and joggled it as if weighing a melon in the market place. 'Mebbe this ain't such a bad assignment after all.'

2

'I cannot abide all those chilli peppers the *peons* use. No wonder they die from diseases of the bowels.' Dona Andrea, as she had introduced herself, was sitting at the head of the banqueting table in the high-vaulted dining-room, dressed in ankle-length black lace over satin, a collar of diamonds at her somewhat wrinkled throat. 'Do you notice the French influence in the cooking here? The Empress Carlotta introduced it. Not that I agreed with them being here. But she and Maximilian did have some civilizing effects on our nation, among the upper classes, at least.'

'Yep, real tasty.' Slaughter scooped up with a *tortilla* the last of the garlic, oregano and tomato sauce that had flavoured the breast of duck. 'If I weren't in polite society I'd lick the plate clean with my tongue.'

'Please feel free,' she smiled. 'What's a tongue for, apart from talking, otherwise?'

'I can think of one or two thangs.' He licked his own tongue through his moustache and stroked it clean. 'Still, I s'pose the *peons* ain't got much choice. They gotta give their *tortillas* some kinda taste. After all, that's generally all they git to eat, or ain't you aware of that?'

Slaughter supped the rich ruby wine in his cut-glass tumbler. Perhaps he'd had too much. It always made him belligerent. He was supposed to be trying to get around this gal. 'This is real friendly of you ma'am. It's sure tastier than that lizard I roasted the day before last.'

'You are an amusing gentleman, Mr Tiffany. Much better company than those boors you saw down in the courtyard. I keep them for protection, not for their conversation. Of course I'm aware of the lot of the *peons*, but they're going to be better off now under our new president, surely? Hasn't he promised them free schools, free hospitals, to divide up the lands of the church and the *haciendados?* They will all have their own little plot.'

'Yep. Easier said than done.' Slaughter reached for a cigar from the humidor on the table, lit one of the sulphur matches that rested in a stone tray, and sucked it alight. 'Mm, real nice.' He leaned back, blew a smoke ring, and watched it float towards the volutes of the ceiling. 'From what I saw of li'l Benito Juarez he's bitten off more than he can chew. He's got queues of peasants waiting with petitions in the corridors of his palace in Mexico City, the generals of his army breathing down his neck, needing their rewards. An' that bloodthirsty bastard Porfirio Diaz waiting in the wings for his chance to become cock of the dungheap.'

'At least the French have been thrown out. Mexico is independent again. You say Maximilian has been executed by firing squad? That is a shock. News travels so slowly up this way.'

'Yep.' Slaughter — under his alias of Frank Tiffany — had given her his hazy lowdown on the political situation as far as he knew, although for the past year he had been bounty-hunting in America. 'Still, if that Austrian fop wanted to set himself up as emperor of a foreign country that was the chance he took.'

'Would you care for any desert, Mr Tiffany?'

'Waal, that depends on what you got to offer?'

Slaughter had been given clean white baggy pants and shirt, the pyjama-like outfit most *peons* wore, with a pair of rope-soled *huavaches*. They were comfortable, but, unarmed, he did not really feel at ease. He wondered how on earth he was going to get his own clothes and guns back. He had finally been forced to forfeit his knife, too. The face at the window bothered him. 'You

26

say the *haciendado* has gone away?'

'Yes, he needs medical treatment. He is not well.'

'So, what's he called?'

'Don Arturo del Briganze de Apuarte. You only have to ask around in outlying villages, they would tell you that.'

'And what is your relationship with him?'

'I am his mistress of the past seventeen years. Or, I was. He is, you could say, past it now. He never married me. To tell you the truth I regard that as an insult. I bitterly resent it, but what can a woman do?'

'Hmm, I dunno.' Slaughter took another puff of the fine green cigar and considered this. 'I guess she cain't do a lot if a guy don't wanna git hitched. She cain't lead him to the altar at gunpoint. Or can she?'

Dona Andrea's dark face spread into a smile, giving a glint of gold where a couple of teeth were replaced, and wreathing her face in laughter wrinkles. 'Should we stop beating

27

about the bush?'

'That depends what bush you're talkin' 'bout.'

'As I said, you've a very amusing man, and an attractive one. I've no idea what goes on in your mind, but your body, I couldn't help noticing, is quite something. Would you be attracted to an older woman, Mr Tiffany?'

'Waal.' The cigar end glowed again as he assessed her. She had plastered her face in some kind of flour paste to lighten its darkness and hide the wrinkles. Her black hair was drawn back and held in a diamond brooch. Her eyebrows had been plucked almost bare. Her eyes were outlined with dark kohl. And her lips were painted red like some whore's. 'I guess I owe you for the meal, ma'am. My guess is you must be old enough to be my mother — God rest her soul — but, sure, I'm attracted to you. Who wouldn't be?'

'That is honest of you to say so. We older women, too, have our needs.'

'Yep.' Slaughter, in fact, had been

with plenty of women older and uglier than her in the shady bordellos and low drinking-holes both sides of the border. In this thirsty land wells were few and far between and a man had to drink where he could. Maybe he could mingle business and pleasure here? 'You want me to be honest? OK, I been with plenty meat-mincers in my time but I ain't come across many as classy as you, Andrea.'

'Thank you, Frank. Somewhat crudely put but I appreciate that sentiment.'

Slaughter had turned his chair to face her, his feet stuck out, watching her in the candlelight. Funnily enough, the more he drank the more attractive she seemed. Suddenly, Dona Andrea slipped across and wound her arm around his neck, sitting on his lap, and touching his lips with hers. 'I adore young, dangerous men like you.'

'Waal, you certainly ain't no blushing flower.' She struck him more like some rattler coiling herself around him, her mouth blowing gently in one ear, her hands everywhere, her tongue licking down his cheek to protrude in between his lips, probing his throat. 'Jeez!' he gasped in an interlude.

He stood, picking her up with him, kissing her some more. Her body was like her face, as sharp and thin as a cut-throat razor. He picked her up and thrust her back over the oak banqueting table, amid the used plates and bowls of succulent peaches, sending cups and bottles crashing.

'Oh, my God!' she gasped. 'I do have a bed, Frank.' But she gripped her thin, whipcord arms tight around his neck. 'Oh, God!'

'The bed can wait 'til later,' he muttered as for several minutes they struggled together. It was more like some harsh battle for supremacy, more like the mating dance of a black widow spider than making love. And for moments it occurred to him that she might do as they did — eat him afterwards.

'Good God!' she repeated, as he

raised himself from her. 'You don't waste much time.'

'Time ain't what I got a lot of,' he grunted, as he stood, and poured himself another drink. 'Where's that bed?'

He serviced her more gently and slowly there for a while and lay back, sweat pouring from him, on the feather mattress of the wide oak double bed.

'That was great, Frank,' she whispered, bending over him. 'Do you really like me?'

'Sure,' he drawled. 'You're jest like an old Kentucky rifle, a good tight fit.'

Dona Andrea laughed, harshly. 'You're an insulting bastard, aren't you? What are you really here for, Frank? What are you up to?'

'I could ask you the same question,' he said.

★   ★   ★

When she suddenly dozed off for a few seconds from exhaustion he whipped a cord from a brocade window cover and,

31

pinning her down with his knees on her shoulders, quickly tied her wrists to the bedposts.

'What are you doing?' she protested, opening her dark eyes, perhaps, at first, thinking he had some game in mind, but then beginning to spit and snarl curses as she realized she was his prisoner. '*Basta!* Let me go!'

'I'm making my move before you make yourn,' he grunted as he secured her kicking legs. 'Too bad, honey.'

Her oaths became more shrill and lurid so he gagged her with her discarded pantalettes. 'Tut, tut! That ain't nice language fer a lady. There's somethang fishy going on in this house and I intend to find out what.'

Slaughter, in his cotton *peon* costume, had no weapon apart from his hands. In the light of the flickering candelabra he studied the naked older woman wriggling and struggling on the bed, trying to gabble through the gag. 'Maybe I oughta choke the life outa you now 'fore you have me killed. But, hell'

— he shrugged a grin — 'how can I do that after your fine hospitality?'

He carefully unlocked the thick oak door and peered out — the *vaquero* in the natty, silver-embroidered outfit was sat on a stool at the end of the corridor, a carbine across his knees. He raised himself, swinging it towards Slaughter, who called back into the room in Spanish, 'I won't be long, *muchacha*. What do you want, wine or whiskey?' He sauntered towards the sharp-faced young man, yawned and scratched his hair. 'We need some more booze. She's red-hot, ain't she? Insatiable. Do all the guests get this treatment?'

The *vaquero* gave a leering smile beneath his sombrero, moving the carbine away. 'Not all of them. She seems to have taken a fancy to you. Come on, I'll show you the cellar.'

'*Gracias.*' Slaughter swiftly caught hold of the carbine barrel and chopped the edge of his right hand hard across the *vaquero*'s jugular. He went down as if pole-axed. 'Sorry about this, *amigo*,' he muttered as he dragged him by his boot-heels back to the bed-chamber. He ripped a sheet and hog-tied the guard with the heels and wrists behind his back. He gagged him with his bandanna as Dona Andrea's fierce eyes watched. 'So long,' he called as he stepped outside and locked the door.

The bounty-hunter picked up the fallen carbine and crept bare-foot around a bend in the corridor to where a tar-flare in an iron holder on the wall threw slopping shadows across a landing. They were on the first floor. There was another floor up above. He heard footsteps approaching from the ground floor banqueting-room. These days he did not care to kill anyone unless he was forced to — he had seen enough killing to last him the rest of his life. Nor did he want to cause a noise that might arouse the house — it was the early hours of morning and most would be asleep. He watched as the big-girthed *vicioso* reached the top of the stone steps. He swivelled around in his greasy leathers and his bloodshot eyes opened wide when he saw Slaughter, who called softly, 'Hi!'

Without hesitation the Mexican went for the pearl-handled revolver tucked in his belt of bullets and had it half-whipped out when the butt of the carbine cracked into his jaw. He coughed a shower of teeth and spun around. Slaughter buffaloed him on the back of his thick neck and he went down with an, 'Ugh!' Out cold. The American bent down and picked up three solid gold teeth. 'Whadda ya know?' He slipped them in his pocket and took the revolver from the unconscious man's hand. It was an eight-inch-barrel Richards conversion of a Colt Navy. Slaughter clicked the cylinder against his ear. 'Hmm. Nice piece. Wonder who he stole this from?'

'Raoul?' a husky voice shouted from the landing above. 'That you? What you playing at? Come on up here, pronto.'

'I drop my damn gun,' Slaughter replied gruffly, cursing colourfully in

Mexican. He laid the carbine aside, put Raoul's extremely wide-brimmed sombrero on his head, grabbed the tar flare in his left, the Richards revolver in his right, and started up the adobe-walled stairway, muttering about how it was too damn dark to see where he was going, keeping his head bent forward so his face wasn't visible. 'Is that *hombre* still in there with her?'

'Yeah, I guess. It's her way of finding out what she wants from a fella. Soon we should have the pleasure of killing him. Unless she's done that already.'

'Not just yet, mister.' Slaughter looked up and saw the bearded American standing at the top of the stairway. He leapt forward and thrust the burning flare in his face.

'Aagh!' The gringo gun-fighter recoiled, knocking the flare away, flapping his hands at his smouldering beard and eyebrows. 'You would, would you?'

He kicked out at Slaughter's groin, but his fellow-Texan dodged the blow, although a vicious spur rowel ripped through his cotton pants high on the thigh. He hurled the flare at his assailant who retreated. They stood three feet apart taking stock of each other. Hatred burned in the older man's eyes as he became aware that the deathly hole of the Richards' business-end was aimed at his heart by a man with a stone-steady hand.

'Right, take your gun out nice 'n easy, forefinger and thumb on the butt, and put it on the floor. Don't try nuthin'. Good. Kick it over to me. Now, turn round and unlock that door.'

'You'll never get away from here.' The de-gunned man fixed him with an angry glare, but unhitched a key ring from his belt and did as he was bid. He swung open the door to reveal an emaciated, silver-haired, elderly man standing centre-floor in a sparsely furnished room. 'You'll never git this ole fool outa here alive, either.'

'You're entitled to your opinion,' Slaughter muttered. 'Step inside.' As the American did so, he cracked the

Richards hard across the nape and he went down. He secured his ankles to his wrists with the man's own belt. 'That should hold him.' He doffed the extravagant sombrero from his head, and bowed to the old man. 'Don Arturo del Briganza de Apuarte? You sent for me?'

'You have identification?' the old man whispered. 'You see, I trust nobody.'

'Sure.' Slaughter took the torn half-page from his wallet. 'This it?'

The frail *haciendado*, attired in flared velvet trousers and a once-expensive but now torn and dirty cambric shirt, went to a bunk on which lay his only reading matter, a Bible. He fitted the half-page to a torn page of Ecclesiastes. 'You're the one I sent for.' He sat on the bunk and looked up at the bounty-hunter. 'I beg you to help me. I am being kept here prisoner in my own home.'

'So I gathered. So, now you're free. What you gonna do, charge these characters with unlawful imprisonment? They been beating up on you?'

He had noticed bruises on the old man's face and his fingers were twisted and bloodstained like they'd tried the thumbscrews on him. In spite of his shocked appearance he still held his head high, the prow of his nose jutting, his long silver hair hanging around his pale features, and he retained a certain aristocratic arrogance.

'That witch trying to make you sign your lands over to her, eh?'

'They have tried, but I have held out. I have told them little. They have not been too cruel because they fear I might die before everything is theirs. Or hers. Andrea was my *mayordomo* for many years.'

'Your lover, too, she said. She thinks she's entitled.'

'That woman is a nymphomaniac. She is any man's lover.'

'Right, that's me included as any man,' Slaughter said. 'But I had the feeling she wanted to know what I am doing here, plying me with wine, food and the rest.'

'You are fortunate she didn't feed you rat poison. She took you to her bed? If you had told her your true reason for being here she would have cut your throat in your sleep. That woman is pure evil.'

'Thanks for warning me, but I kinda guessed she wasn't all purity and light. Still, she ain't so bad in the sack.'

The *haciendado* frowned. 'For many years I did not suspect her cheating. I would have left her a good piece of my fortune. But she wants everything. So I have vowed she will have nothing.'

'So, what gives? You want me to git you outa here?'

'No, I am too old, too weak to ride far. I want you to find someone for me. I am ashamed to tell you that when I was younger I behaved badly. In my forties I married a beautiful young girl, but, being set in my ways, I carried on in my usual style.'

'Taking advantage of your feudal rights to the local girls?'

'Yes, not excessively, but it was wrong

of me. My wife left me, escaped from this house while I was absent, taking our baby daughter with her. I have regretted it ever since. You see before you a broken and lonely old man.'

'You want me to find your ex-wife, your daughter, is that it, so that they can inherit?'

'Yes, there is more than this house and lands at stake: there is a cache of silver worth a fortune. I used to have a mine at Durango. With all the revolutionary fervour of the past years, the War of Independence, I did not trust banks. I hid the silver in the deserted mine for a rainy day. That day is now.'

'You mean you want me to make sure your wife and daughter get your little nest egg?'

'Yes. I am not sure my wife is alive. I heard a rumour she died in the cholera epidemic. My daughter would be about twenty now. I have not seen her since she was two years old, but in my memory, I love her dearly. I believe she was in a convent, Our Lady of

Guadaloupe, but now they are being disbanded by the revolutionaries I am at a loss to know where she might be.'

'Yeah?' Slaughter pursed his lips. 'Sounds like I'll be looking fer a needle in a haystack. This is gonna take time.'

'I fear I have no spare cash to make you an advance. They stole it from me.'

'Yeah? That's not a good start. I don't work cheap. You give me details of this mine, how you know I ain't gonna run off with the whole caboodle, anyhow?'

'You fought for Juarez. I heard about you, that you are an honourable man, if a trifle bitter, perhaps. There is something unfortunate in your past, like mine, that haunts you, makes you unable to settle down. I have heard that for the right price you are a man who gets a job done.'

'Waal, I try.'

'So, I trust you. Your payment will be a quarter share. A quarter goes to my wife, a quarter to my daughter, and a quarter to me.'

'Of how much?'

'Silver worth a quarter of a million pesos.'

'Whoo!' Slaughter gave a low whistle. 'I wonder where she hid my pants? The sooner I git started the better it will be. I'll take your offer, Don Arturo. Maybe I'll be back, maybe not. We'll see. If I don't succeed I get no fee, that it?'

'Yes, but there is another thing: you must go quickly and secretively. My fear is that these fiends will follow you and kill my daughter to prevent her inheriting.'

'Maybe I oughta kill Andrea before I go, that might simplify things.'

'As bad as she is, I cannot authorize you to do that.'

'Nope. An' I ain't in the habit of murdering a lady I just dallied with. I gotta think of my reputation! What about you? What you gonna do?'

'I will stay here, their prisoner. I will tell them that as I had no cash for a down payment you have refused to help and gone home. Andrea will try to force me to marry her but I will refuse. Don't worry about me. Go, *señor*, with all speed before they manage to get free.'

'That kid who summoned me here, how's he fit into this?'

Don Arturo glanced at the unconscious man on the floor and hissed, 'Manolo is my illegitimate son by one of the serving girls. He has grown up here. I am fond of him. He will be remembered in my will if you succeed. But tell no one or he, too, will be killed.'

'Yeah? They really are evil, huh? OK.' He stuck out his hand and shook with the *haciendado*. 'It's a deal. I'll do what I can.'

Slaughter gave the *Americano* another thump across the skull, because he was beginning to stir, then hurried down through the sleeping house. He found his pants, shirt and jeans hanging on a line and pulled them on. His boots were in the bath-house. He found his knife and guns in a room used as a bunkhouse by the guards, and buckled on his gunbelt.

44

He was just in the act of doing this when the guard from the tower, Jaime, appeared in the doorway, calling out, 'Hold it!'

Slaughter spun around, seeing in a split second that Jaime had his carbine covering him, his finger on the trigger. He went for his Schofield, jumping to one side as the carbine barked, and he had it out and crashing lead faster than a man could blink. Jaime pirouetted and tumbled over a table hanging limp. Slaughter pulled his head up by his hair. He was dead.

'Shee-it!' he sighed. 'How did I manage to fergit about you? I must be losing my touch.

'No,' he chuckled, as he picked up the carbine. 'I guess Dona Andrea plumb wore me out.'

Slaughter edged out of the house. *Peons* were shouting and calling, aroused by the gunshots, but there didn't appear to be anybody else dangerous about. He crossed to the stables where a groom roused from his sleep in the hay got to his feet, his hands high. 'Don't kill me, señor.'

'I ain't planing to. Jest git me my black mustang saddled. I got a few thangs to do.'

When he returned the horse was waiting and the groom creaked open the big gate to let him out. '*Gracias.*' Slaughter swung aboard and tossed him a gold tooth as a tip. 'Don't show it to Raoul, he might object. *Adios.*' He pulled the mustang around, raked his sides and sent him pounding away across the desolate valley which was streaked a ghostly white and blue by the moonlight. 'Hey-ya!' he shouted. 'We're free.'

3

'What are you staring at me for, man?' Dona Andrea shrieked. 'Untie me.'

The bearded American, Jake Scullock, had been the first to struggle free from his bonds as Don Arturo watched, making no move to assist him. Scullock had slapped some life into the swarthy, recumbent Raoul and, with the help of a couple of *peons* and a stout corral post, had managed to batter open the door of Andrea's locked bed-chamber. Scullock gave the naked woman straddled across the bed a shifty grin, half-tempted to ride her, himself, but he cut her free.

'What's the matter, haven't you seen a woman before?' Andrea snatched up a blanket to cover herself. 'What are you, *schoolboys*? You let that man take you all apart.'

'Well, you don't seem to have done

so well, yourself,' Jake muttered, kneeling to free the gagged and bound, slim Mexican, Ygenio Guttierez. 'He jumped us.'

'He took my gold teeth,' Raoul Yerby roared, holding his aching jaw and poking a finger tenderly at the bloody gaps. 'When I catch up with the lousy gringo I'm going to tie him to the ant-heap and watch him being eaten alive.'

'First I will castrate him and cut off the soles of his feet so that the blood flows,' Guttierez snarled, brushing dust from his snappy outfit and pushing fingers through his black curls. 'Hey, what he done with our guns?'

'Don Arturo will suffer for this. It is he must have summoned him here. Has he gone with him?'

'No, I locked him back in his room,' Scullock growled to the woman's questions. 'What we gonna do now?'

'What you think? Go find your guns, saddle your horses and get after him. Get out of here while I dress.'

'You mean you want him killed?'

'Of course I want him killed.'

'Maybe that ain't such a bright idea,' Jake Scullock said. 'Maybe Don Arturo has told him something like where that hoard of silver is you figure he's gotten hidden, where to find his daughter? Maybe it'd be best to let him lead us to 'em and then kill them?'

'You're right.' Dona Andrea glanced at Scullock with a new respect. 'I was letting my anger rule my brain. There will be leisure to kill him later. I am glad one of you three has some sense.'

She was dressed in a purple blouse, bandanna, split leather riding skirt, polished boots and a straight-brimmed, low-crowned black hat when Scullock appeared on the landing again.

'He's taken all our guns. He ain't so dim. No doubt he's ditched 'em in the rocks someplace. All we can find is one lousy shotgun. Jaime's dead, too.'

'Jaime? Damn that gringo! No matter. We can buy more guns at the first town we come to. Get the groom to saddle my horse. I'm coming with you.'

'You're coming with us?' the middle-aged American echoed, disbelievingly.

'You don't think I'm going to let you three get your sticky fingers on that silver, do you?' she snapped, picking up a rawhide riding quirt and slapping it against her boot. 'You men work for me and you'd better not forget it.'

'There ain't no use talking like that,' Jake Scullock growled. 'That's askin' fer trouble. You gotta trust us. But, I tell you somethang' — he jabbed a forefinger at her — 'I wan' a good share of whatever we come up with. You and me's goin half-shares on the main prize, sister, and don't you fergit it. You can fob them other two monkeys off with a coupla thousand pesos. All they need is enough to get drunk 'n laid. Me, I got plans for my retirement.'

'You'll get your share.'

He caught Andrea by her wrist in a strong grip. 'I said half-share. You better remember that. And you can fergit the phoney *Dona* bit. To me you ain't no lady. You're jest some damn leathery Mex hoo-er. So, don't try none of your tricks.'

'Let me go! How dare you?' When he did so, she rubbed her wrist, gave him a false smile, purring, 'Don't you worry, Jake. I wouldn't try to pull anything over a man like you. Half-shares it is. You and I we are partners. The other two? Pah! They have no brains. They are dispensable.'

'Good,' he said. 'Just as long as you remember that.'

'Come on.' She picked up a woollen poncho, blanket roll, and a bag of travel equipment she had packed. 'We will keep on his tail, but we will stay behind him. I won't hold you up. I can ride as well as any man. I will leave the servants to tend to Don Arturo under penalty of death should he escape.'

★　★　★

He pushed the black mustang at a steady lope through the ravines of

51

vermilion cliffs following the trickle of the Santa Maria river in the shimmering noontide heat. When he paused to let his horse drink, he knelt down and filled his leather hat with the muddy water, glancing around him at the harsh outline of the crags through his narrowed eyes, always on the *qui vivre*, as they say. It wasn't Apache he feared — they skulked up in the higher reaches of the mountains — it was *bandidos*, gangs of lowdowns who roamed these hills, who had used the revolution as an excuse to line their own pockets, and who would gladly slit a man's throat for a couple of pesos. But there was little sign of life in this remote region. He supped the water, trying to filter it through his teeth in order to drain out the sediment, spitting out mud and grit. A man needed water in this heat, well above 110 degrees on Fahrenheit's scale. He gathered the reins and swung with lithe ease back into the saddle.

Slaughter nudged the mustang forward with his knees and chuckled as he remembered how he had gathered up their carbines and revolvers in a burlap sack and tossed it off a cliff. He felt a little safer for that. On a ridge, he bent the horse around and paused, peering back into the haze, but if they were coming there was no sign of them. He pushed onwards. He had a long way to go to Durango, a six- or seven-day ride.

It was an unwelcoming land, where what animals there were, diamond-backed rattlers, chuckawallah lizards, ground squirrels, mangey foxes, the occasional puma, or even rarer black jaguar, were involved in the daily struggle to survive. Only the little hummingbirds seemed happy to be alive as they hovered to suck the nectar from the brilliant yellow cactus flowers among spikey clumps of Spanish bayonet, mesquite, and the tortuously shaped Agaves.

Slaughter rode through it all, his steed slowly eating up the miles. At night he would find a sandy patch to sleep, build a small fire of dry twigs to boil up his coffee, roast whatever he could catch, a quail, lizard, or lowly field rat, and bake a flapjack in the ashes. He had grown accustomed over the years to living off the land, and did so with the same stoic acceptance as his Comanche forebears. He would wrap himself in his leather coat, a blanket around his knees, carbine tucked between them, revolver nestled in his loins, hunting knife dug in the sand close at hand, and pull his hat over his eyes to cut out the bright moonlight as he slept, waking, suddenly alert, at the slightest sound. Usually it was just some nocturnal animal predator scuttling its butt around. But out there a man never knew who might creep up on him or lie in wait.

He had already passed the dusty plaza and boxy 'dobes of the ramshackle town of Modero, ragged, barefoot men and women silently watching him, like the vulture sitting on a roof watched him, too. Rib-thin dogs and naked children stood, flies buzzing at their eyes. The new constitution didn't seem to have done a lot for them just yet. But it was good to slake his thirst with a rusty beer from a tin barrel, in a shady *pulqueria* colourfully named *The Daughters of Eve*.

'If that's the best Eve can do,' he muttered, glancing across at a dark and skinny, cross-eyed whore, 'God help her.'

God, of course, was banned now in this land. The mission church was barred and closed. The priest had been put up against a wall and shot. A patch of bloodstain on the paving and a faded bunch of lilies marked the spot. Wooden-faced older women in their black *rebozos*, the all-purpose shawl, shopping bag, baby-carrier and nose-wiper, sat and counted their rosary beads, nonetheless. He ate a tortilla of grilled grasshoppers, and a crisp chunk of roasted pig-skin, and rode on his way. A soldier of the revolution sat listlessly in his hot uniform outside his office and watched him pass, but he did not intervene. Some of these *Yanqui* sage rats, he knew, could be a mite touchy and quick on the trigger. It was too hot for trouble.

Out past the ornate tombs of the cemetery. Mexico! It would never change, he thought, in spite of all the wars they fought.

'Come on, hoss,' he grunted, giving a prick of the spurs. 'Let's move, shall we?'

* * *

He was two days out of Modero, back in the vast emptiness of the upland plateau, when he came to a narrow ravine that led into a range of hills blocking his route. There was no distinct trail to follow. His method of navigation was to head due south guided by the sun, which, mid-afternoon, was beginning its westerly fall. 'Looks like we might find a way up through here,' he said. 'Come on, boy.'

He urged his mount up through

scattered boulders, some higher than his head, tumbled haphazardly. He let him pick his own way through the vicious pin-cushions of cholla cactus which could poison the mustang's legs if any barbs were not picked out. Up they climbed through a steep slope of organ cactus following a narrow defile. He was glad of the *tapaderos* shielding his own legs from the thorns. It was odd how the tiny cactus wren lived among it all with impunity and immunity.

There was something sinister about this ravine, or, what was it, a tingling of the hairs at the back of his neck that told him he didn't want to die just yet? The instinct that warned him of danger was confirmed when he saw a wren whirr from its nest in a clump of cholla higher up in the canyon. Without hesitation he leaped from his mustang and dragged him into the cover of a rock as a rifle barked out and chiselled rock where, a semi-second before, his head had been.

'Jeez!' he cried, grabbing his carbine from the boot. 'We've run into an ambush.'

That was a tad obvious because all hell had broken out, rifle fire crackling through the chaparal, bullets smashing and ricocheting through cactus and rocks all about them. The flashes of gunfire showed about twenty gunmen were ranged in a semi-circle up above him. At least, that was as far as he could tell as lead whined about his head, forcing him to duck back into cover. He crawled to another position, raised himself, levered a slug into the Winchester and took aim at one of the flashes of fire.

'Ough!' a man shouted, angrily, as if he might have stubbed his toe. But he slithered from his hiding place, a rifle still gripped in his hands, and rolled over to lie still, bleeding from the bullet in his chest. That gave them pause.

There was an uncanny silence as black powdersmoke drifted through the sunny ravine. 'Hey *gringo*,' a shrill voice wheedled. 'You keel my *amigo*. Why you do that? That not nice.' The taunting voice erupted into cackling laughter. 'We got you surrounded,' he sang out. 'But we don' wan' keel you. All we wan' is your monnay. Come out weeth your han's up an' geev us what you got an', thass OK, we let you go. OK?'

'Huh! Some hope. No, it ain't OK.'

He sent five slugs in fast succession at the clump of cactus from which the voice had come, shredding it, and there was a yelp of fear, which provoked another rattle of gunfire from all quarters. Slaughter jumped back beside the mustang, resting his back against the big rock. Well, at least, they weren't soldiers, just a pack of lousy bandits. And their aim wasn't so hot. But how long he could hold out here was doubtful against such a number. They were keeping hidden and playing, they thought, like cats with a mouse.

'Show yourself, *hombre*, and I'll toss you my wallet,' Slaughter shouted. 'I ain't got a lot, but what there is you're welcome to. Then go your ways and I'll go mine.'

'Hey, no,' the jeering voice replied. 'You theenk I'm crazy? You show yourself meester, then we talk business.'

'Damn you.' Slaughter stood and aimed the carbine at the shadowy figure behind his rock. There was a scream this time and a bandit beside the spokesman threw up his arms and toppled back. Slaughter ducked back as another fusillade began. 'Got another of the bastards.'

But in another lull in the interchange of lead the *bandido* who spoke frontier English was still there and taunting: 'You keel another of my frien's, greengo. That not good. Now we can no be nice to you.' Whoever he was he gave a giggle of laughter and shouted out instructions in Spanish for various of his men to close in. 'When we catch you, greengo, you goin' haff to die very slowly. How many bullets you got left? We can wait for you.'

A good question. Slaughter reloaded the Winchester, concentrating, with deft experience, poking twelve into the magazine. Twelve left in his belt, six trusty friends in his Schofield, but would it be enough to fend them off? He somehow doubted it. Maybe it would be best to take a chance and make a break, send the mustang galloping hell for leather out of there. But, wouldn't a chase be more to their liking?

'Aw, damn you to hell,' he shouted, at whoever it was up there jeering and laughing at him. 'Come and get it. Do your worst. Earn your damn pay.'

Slaughter stood up, his blood pounding, the murderous impulse of the hunter strong in him, crazily angry, full of the killer instinct that came naturally to him, jumping from behind the rock, facing them, levering slugs and shooting in one sustained volley of sound, traversing his aim around in a semi-circle, taking them by surprise, sending them diving for cover, no time to think, everything split-second, bam-crack, bam-crack!

The Mexicans were yelling and blazing away, one man falling to his knees clutching his gut, another's chest gouging blood, a third with blood running down his face grabbing for his eyes, and a fourth leaping like a scalded cat and rolling down the slope. Slaughter began jumping from side to side, scrambling up towards them through the rocks, shooting at everything that moved, first time, no chance to take careful aim. And *there* was another one sent flying into Eternity.

But an ominous click told him his magazine was empty and he rolled behind a shallow rock as bullets spattered and ploughed around him. It was a miracle he was still alive. The line of an army song drummed into his mind,

' . . . trust to your luck,
And march to your front like a soldier.'

His face split into a grim grin. 'Yeah. Here goes.' He pulled out his revolver, cocking it with his thumb, preparing for another charge on the enemy, one which this time must be into certain death. It would be like charging a firing squad.

'Greengo, you are a brave man but you haff no chance.' The shrill jeering voice curdled into him. 'Come on, try again. Maybe you be lucky.'

Lucky Slaughter must have been, for suddenly another rifle shot cracked out from higher up the hill-side and one of the *bandidos* was propelled spinning and sliding out of cover to lie on his back, dead. For the first time Slaughter saw the leader of the bandits, a tall skinny man with protuberant, crooked teeth, his hair lank beneath a peaked cap, who was forced to jump out from his rock to the cover of the other side as a fusillade of bullets poured down on him and his men from two points on the hillsides. He had presented himself as a clear target, but Slaughter was as surprised as he was, and, with bullets ricocheting and whining about his own ears, he did not take advantage of the opportunity.

Instead, he watched with fascinated horror as the lead from the marksmen up above ploughed with unfailing accuracy into backs and bodies, and a Mexican's head was splattered like a cantaloupe melon.

'*Hombres, vamos!*' their chief shrieked, and wasted no time in following his own advice, leaping and dodging through the rocks towards a sheltered gully on one side where they had obviously left their horses. Only about four of his men managed to scramble after him, for now Slaughter was fanning his hammer to mow down another three of them. When his redhot revolver was empty he could only watch as the two snipers up above cut the gang to smithereens. He saw the leader, mounted, whipping his mustang out of there. The last bandit who tried to follow was hit by a rifle shot, toppled from the saddle as he reached the crest.

There was an uneasy silence as his rescuers surveyed the scene — at least fifteen bandits lying dead or wounded among the rocks as a pall of black powdersmoke drifted.

'Who the hell are they?' Slaughter wondered.

And then there was a booming voice from up in the rocks and a big-bellied, gap-toothed man, stepped out of cover, grinning. 'They had enough? Is that the lot of them?'

'Swanger! Well, I'll be damned. Where you come from?'

'We was just passing and heard the commotion. Is that you, Slaughter? You ole hard-ass. If I'd a known it was you I'd've let 'em kill you.'

He jumped down through the scrub, finishing off a groaning man with a pistol shot, as if it were an everyday occurrence. And a ferrety-faced little man in nuggety homespun appeared to one side of the ravine, his longarm at the ready.

'Abel? Abel Funt? You still ridin' with that li'l runt?'

'Aw, he's OK,' Seth Swanger beamed. 'He cain't help being a touch dim up top. But he kin shoot the eye out of a squirrel, I tell you that, boy.'

'Yeah, so I saw. You arrived, like they say, in the nick of time. I owe ya.'

'You sure do, Slaughter,' Abel called, finishing another Mexican who was attempting to raise his revolver. 'You woulda bin dead meat.'

'Never thought you two would turn out to be my guardian angels. Thanks, boys.'

'What's brought you down to this God-forsaken country again? I thought you was up in the States,' Swanger said, as Slaughter brushed himself down with his hat, and shook his black hair from his eyes. 'You wouldn't be riding this way if you wasn't planning on earning some bounty. I know you, Slaughter. How about counting us in?'

'Boys, I like Mexico. It's my home from home,' Slaughter grinned. 'I'm just on a little holiday.'

'Yeah, tell us another,' Abel Funt whined.

'Waal, call it romance. I'm going to see a ladyfriend of mine.'

Swanger watched Slaughter sliding his last few slugs into the cylinder of his big Schofield revolver and going to pick up a bandolier of bullets from a fallen bandit, tossing it over his shoulder.

'You're a lying, crafty sonuvabitch. What's ticking behind that leathery mug of yourn? You got something on, I can smell it.'

'Boys, we was good companions in the wars, both of 'em. You've looked out for me this time, and I thank you. Jest look at these scumbags. There's no use feeling any pity for them. Now they're dead, and I'm alive, so I'll be headin' on my way. I work on my own, you know that.'

'You might have been a loner so far,' Swanger said, slapping him mightily on the back, 'but now you're part of a threesome. OK? We're with you, boy.'

Abel was busy hopping from corpse to corpse, going through pockets, prising out gold teeth with his knife. 'Hey, look what I got,' he cried, holding up a silver crucifix. 'Fancy him carrying such a thang.'

'Waal, I guess,' Swanger said, 'even these stupid galoots got mamas someplace who'll be praying for 'em.'

'Looks like their prayin' ain't done 'em much good,' Slaughter muttered. 'We won this one, boys.'

4

'It was real providential bumping into you like that.' Swanger beamed and pulled his blanket around his shoulders, leaning back against a rock, warmed by the blaze of their camp-fire. 'The Lord musta guided our feet.'

'Providential fer *him*,' Abel Funt cried. 'He owes us.'

'Yeah, so you keep telling me.' Slaughter cupped his hands around a tin mug of hot coffee and gave a scoffing laugh. Sure, he was grateful to them for their intervention, glad to be alive, but, on the other hand, he wondered how he was going to get rid of them. If he just got on his bronc and rode off they would be sure to follow. In the meantime, Abel had insisted on rounding up the dead *bandidos'* horses and herding them along with them. The dust they kicked up would alert anyone following. He had also picked up all their guns and ammunition and packed them on the back of one of the mustangs. He didn't believe in wasting anything. Now he was carefully counting out all the pesos and small valuables he had taken from the Mexicans' pockets, his rifle across his knees, his hatchet face concentrating hard as he sorted them into little piles.

'You planning on splitting that among us?'

'Sure I am. We're all *compadres*, ain't we?' Abel hooted. 'We took that gunboat on the Tennessee River, didn't we? We were with Forrest on the raid into Memphis, weren't we? Whoo! That sure made them Yankees shee-it their pants.'

'That commander of the city, what was his name, General Washburn, he didn't have no pants to shee-it into. We chased him in his 'cutty sarks' as he sprinted half a mile to safety. Still, we took his uniform as a trophy. That musta hurt his pride.' Swanger chuckled, with his wicked, gappy grin. 'I could never understand why the gen'ral gave it back, nor them top-brass prisoners, neither. I'd'a slit their throats.'

'Aw, he was a gen'l'man, the gen'ral. Them sort at the top they stick together,' Abel whined, aggrievedly. 'You know, when we was besieging Fort Pillow on the Mississippi and we was having a fine ole time potting all them black soldiers that ran into the river to try to escape? Well, I saw Forrest shoot some of our own men down to stop the fray. An' him a slaver, too. There he was saving the damn blacks.'

'He was a strange man,' Swanger mused. 'But he did more'n his share of killin'. He was always the first to leap his hoss across the barricades. Christ, he had twenty-nine chargers shot from under him!'

'Glory, allelu-yah!' Abel yelled. 'God save the South.'

Slaughter sighed, for he had heard it all before. He had been with these two all through the Big War, part of the Texas Brigade aligned with Forrest's guerillas. All the way through Kentucky and Tennessee and down through Alabama covering the retreat to Selma, bloody and weary, fighting to the bitter end. And then, like many other Texans, they had refused to accept the surrender and formed a regiment to go off to fight as mercenaries for Juarez. Another four years of hard fighting as they freed Mexico.

And there he was, a year afterwards, still ruthlessly killing all who got in his way. But there was no longer any romantic cause to stir the blood. It was just killing for killing's sake. And the killing of fifteen men that day lay heavy on his heart.

'Ah, hell.' He spat into the flames. 'They were a bunch of low, brutal, cruel, lazy, depraved, blasphemous, ignorant and insolent miscreants . . . '

'Who you talkin' about — Forrest's boys?'

'No, them damn *bandidos*. Lead was the only remedy. I told 'em to leave me alone and be on their way. I even offered to toss 'em my wallet. Some men just don't see sense.'

'Heck!' Swanger boomed with laughter, and squirted a stream of *aguardiente* from a goatskin into his mouth. 'You goin' soft or somethang?' He tossed the vessel of liquor at Slaughter. 'Here, put some fire in ya belly.'

'I'm just sick of killing, thassall,' Slaughter said, tipping his head back and spurting a jet. 'This is my last trip.'

'Yeah?' Swanger's beady eyes brightened in the firelight. 'Then you must be after somethang big. Abel, we stick with him we gonna git rich.'

'Perish the thought, boys. You'd do better to head on back to Texas. All you'll git with me is a bellyful of trouble. It's my middle name.'

'Funny,' Swanger grinned. 'I thought that was Rest-in-Peace. Ain't that what you allus said when you shot a fella? Doncha worry, Loo-tenant, we're gonna stick to you like glue.'

'Lieutenant? Huh! It's a long time since I been called that.' He grabbed the goatskin from Abel and poured some more firewater down his throat. 'Waal, if you two are planning on coming along you better be ready to take orders. I'm in charge of this party. You do what I tell you, there might be some profit come your way.'

'Thass the spirit, Lootenant. Now you're talking. You know it makes sense. Three guns is better'n one in this territory.'

'Yeah,' Slaughter growled, lying back to sleep. 'Maybe.'

* * *

The rising sun sent crimson streamers of light flickering across the vast emptiness of the upland plateau flushing the great pallisades of the distant *cordilleras* in a haze of pink and purple.

'Come on, if you're coming,' he called, kicking the bootsoles of his hungover *hombres*. 'Let's make the most of the dawn cool. Soon this land will be another baking inferno.'

Swanger and Funt grumbled as they hastily boiled up coffee and held their pounding heads. They rounded up their remuda of mustangs, still loose-saddled, and, cracking their lariats, set them trotting on their way.

'Why you gotta bring this mob with you?' Swanger complained to Abel. 'I'm sick of eating their dust.'

But they drove the score of horses on before them through the morning until the sun rose high, burning like a fiery lozenge in the sky. 'Whew! This damned country sure sweats the wet out of a man,' Swanger said, as they paused to take swigs of lukewarm water from their canteens, carefully rationing it, unsure when they might reach a well. 'It's that hot.'

'Aw, quit moanin',' Slaughter muttered. 'You might jest sweat off some of that beer-belly flab on your girth.'

'Thass solid muscle.' Swanger braced himself and punched a fist into his guts. 'Well, what ain't has been paid fer in solid cash. A lot of alcohol's gone into the makin' of my physique.'

'Save your breath,' Slaughter grunted. 'Let's move.'

From then on the only sounds in the midday silence were the thudding of hooves, the jingle of spurs and harness, the rasping breath and indignant snorting of the mustangs as they were driven on. 'Yip! Yip! Yip!' Abel yelled.

Slaughter was riding one of the bandits' scrubby horses to give his big black mustang a rest. Occasionally he would draw in and let the beasts nuzzle water from his palm. They were dangerously overheated. 'Aw, Gawd!' He tipped a last drip from his canteen. 'Thass the water gone.' He eyed distant, dark, copper-coloured clouds easing up over a hill. 'I don't like the look of that.'

'If it's rain an' it's wet I'm all for it.'

'Looks more like a storm to me, Mr Swanger. You ever heard of the Devil Wind? It hits round these parts. It's worse than the twisters we get at home.'

'Devil Wind! Pah! That's a story to

frighten the schoolkids. Come on. What we waiting for?'

They rode on through a barren windgap and, as they reached a rise, Slaughter held up his hand to slow them. 'Riders coming,' he called.

'Who you figure they are?'

'Hell knows.'

Out of a wavering heat mist, a band of riders was approaching and it was difficult to deduce their purpose. They were more like a mirage of ghosts. Slaughter shucked his Winchester out of its greased saddle boot and it came as easy as a bean from its pod. He levered a slug down the spout, resting the carbine across his knees. 'You ready, boys?'

'We sure are.' Swanger and Abel casually hefted their guns. 'Just give the word.'

But it was something of an anti-climatic relief that as they came nearer the riders were seen to be a ragged caravan of traders, men riding, women and children straggling along on foot.

'Let's go parley,' Slaughter said, nudging his mustang forwards with his knees. 'Let's see if they got any water to sell.'

The band of tatterdemalions came to a halt and dark eyes in sullen Indian faces watched them suspiciously. The leading *zacatero* was a tad better attired in a grimy shirt and greasy cowhide pants. He held a big sombrero over his pommel, shading his hands.

'*Buenas*,' Slaughter drawled as he drew near. 'Would you mind putting your hat on? We like to see what a man's got in his fists.'

'You do not trust me, *señor*?'

'We don't trust nobody,' Abel whined. 'Just show your hands nice 'n slow.'

The *zacatero* grinned as the men behind him laughed. But he removed the hat to one side to show that he did, indeed, hold an ancient revolver in his right. He carefully pointed it to one side.

'Right. That's better. Where you come from?'

'Durango. Three days back. You

cannot miss the way. And where are you going, señors, with all those horses?'

Slaughter was wondering if any of the other muleteers were secreting guns. There were a dozen of them; a villainous-looking bunch, but most men were in these parts. He did not relish a fight. It would be a messy operation with women and children about.

'What do you do?' he asked in Spanish.

'We buy, we sell,' the zacatero replied. 'Wax from the candellila plant, rope from the lechugilla. You want to trade, señor?'

'You got any of them wimmin for sale?' Swanger asked.

'Act sensible, if you can,' Slaughter said, eyeing a mule loaded with two wooden barrels. 'We ain't in need of women.'

'Speak for yourself,' Abel crowed.

'Would that be water in them barrels, friend? You sell us one?'

The zacatero's eyes lit up. 'Water is precious, eh? More precious than gold.

We trade you one barrel for all those horses.'

'Hang on!' Abel yelled. 'I ain't selling my hosses for a lousy barrel of water. Thass daylight robbery.'

'You'll do what you're told. The damn horses are a pain in the butt, anyway. I'm sick of driving 'em. Or would you rather die of thirst in this desert?'

Abel licked his dry lips. 'Aw, please your damn self.'

The *zacatero* had caught hold of the big black mustang's bridle, grinning with pleasure at the stupidity of the *gringos*.

'Not that one,' Slaughter said, levering his carbine. 'He's mine. We been together a long time. We're like an old married couple. You just tie one of them water barrels to his saddle and the rest are yourn.'

The *zacatero* grimaced with displeasure, but, noting the way the carbine was aimed unerringly at his heart, he ordered one of the women to do as Slaughter bid.

'Just a moment. I wanna taste it first.'

The woman turned a spigot on the barrel and filled a wooden cup. Slaughter took a swallow. 'Yep, it's good. *Muchas gracias, muchachos.* We'll be on our way.'

'What about all the guns?' Abel asked.

'Aw, let 'em have 'em. They ain' no damn use to us,' Swanger growled. 'You got the soul of a shopkeeper, Abel.'

'They ain't having my guns,' Abel screeched and snatched at the reins of the horse loaded with the bandits' arms. 'They're worth a hundred dollars to me in Durango.'

The Mexicans shrugged and went on their way well pleased with the horses.

'He's got a mind of his own, ain't he, the li'l fella?' Slaughter grinned at Swanger and they set off after Abel. 'C'mon, let's go.'

5

Sister Angostina de Encarnacion, as she had been called before renouncing her vows, was a handsome young woman with astonishingly Scandinavian looks, ice-blue eyes and blonde hair. Her mother had been one of the well-born inhabitants of Gaudalajara, descended from northern Spaniards who had Goth blood, carefully guarded through the centuries, for such women were much-prized in a land where most were dark-haired and dark-eyed. When her mother had married Don Arturo del Briganza de Apuarte her daughter, Angostina, had fortunately inherited her looks.

Or, perhaps, not so fortunately, Angostina sometimes thought, for the blessing of beauty sometimes brought with it much trouble, mainly in the form of harassment by men. Sometimes she wished she could be plain and dumpy and left to get on with her life as she wished to. It had been OK when she was a nun and protected by the uniform and enclosure of the order, but now she had put aside the cowl and wimple and was a plain citizen of the new Mexico she received much unwanted attention.

Angostina thought these thoughts as she waited among a crowd of scruffy *peons* in a corridor of a former colonial mansion in the town of Santa Julia which had been turned into a town hall when the revolutionaries evicted its rich owners. Similar properties in the main street had been taken over and given to the peasants as rooming-houses and were now crowded with families, their chickens, dogs, turkeys, and even donkeys in most unsanitary conditions. It was their squabbles about the delegation of land and houses that had brought most of those present here with their petitions. The ideology of equality propounded by the revolutionaries overlooked one aspect: human greed.

Although Angostina tried to play down her looks by wearing a shabby grey dress and woollen shawl wrapped around her head and shoulders, her vivid eyes and glimpse of her golden hair still caught men's attention, as did her lissom figure — for she found it difficult to disguise the female dimensions that protruded most firmly in the places men preferred them to protrude.

'It's a nuisance,' she hissed, more to herself than to the irate little woman beside her who was complaining. 'He keeps us waiting hours.'

He was the *jefe politico*, Arsenio Romero, appointed to supervise the new revolutionary order in the area and the most powerful of the small band of *anti-Christs*, the soldiers sent to patrol the town and its outlying areas and hunt down any remaining insurgents or hidden priests.

And *he* was the reason why that morning Angostina had a sick sensation in her stomach for she had come to ask why her promised allowance for the orphanage had not been paid. She had a good idea of what his reply would be.

Angostina had become a novice at the Convent of the Sacred Heart of Our Lady of Gaudaloupe at the age of thirteen after her mother had died in a cholera epidemic. The big stone building stood on the edge of Lake Santa Julia some miles out of town. As the War of Independence raged, the nuns had opened their doors to war orphans of both sides. But when the French retreated in disorder as the Juaristas' hordes attacked, there had been panic among the nuns who had heard rumours of rape, killing and burning at other orders. They had been offered the chance of passage on a ship with the French back to Rome and most, including the mother superior, had jumped at it. Only Angostina and two elderly nuns had refused to leave the children. They had chosen to stay and face the oncoming army.

Perhaps it was fortunate that President Benito Juarez himself had paused at the convent by the lake on his triumphant march south to Mexico City. The little Indian had been placid and polite to the nuns amid all the noise of his soldiery, their horses and cannons, as they made camp in the environs. Angostina had responded in kind, providing a meal for him and his officers, and making the mother superior's own bedchamber ready for him to stay the night. Juarez had called her before him to be questioned and Angostina had begged him to think of the orphans, proposing that she be allowed to turn the building into an official orphanage, provided she were guaranteed funds to support it. She had been surprised by her own forwardness for she had rarely spoken to any man since the age of thirteen, let alone a president. Juarez had smiled and said he would agree to her request on one condition: she must abandon her vows and solemnly promise never to preach a word of what he called 'superstitious Catholic nonsense' to any of the children. Angostina had pursed her lips and shook her head and asked if she could give her reply in the morning.

All night she had prayed and wrestled with her conscience, her mind tangled with guilt. How could she deny the existence of God? But there were also other voices. It had to be admitted that for all its wealth, pomp and ceremony, the church had shown little regard for the welfare of the poor and downtrodden in Mexico. In spite of being an unbeliever, Juarez had some strangely Christ-like ideas about helping others. By morning she had made up her mind: she would abandon her vows to help the children. The other two nuns agreed with her. Juarez was pleased, promised she would be given the necessary financial allowance, wished her good fortune and went on his way with his army.

All had gone well in the year since. Once Juarez was established back in power, the money had begun to be allotted to her. It was not much, but enough to pay for food, clothing, bedding, school books and equipment for their small clinic. But, recently, for no apparent reason, the money had dried up. Or, perhaps, she had already guessed the reason and it was that that made her sick to her stomach as she waited there.

Gradually the queue of supplicants was dealt with and her turn arrived. Angostina was ushered in by an armed guard to the main room of the former mansion. He, Arsenio Romero, was seated behind a long oak refectory table on which was a jumble of maps and papers. He was a mestizo, more Indian than Spanish, but his dark skin had been diluted into a sallow yellow colour by some questionable mating. He was thin, with more of a Chinese look than Mexican, but plenty of that race flourished in the coastal ports. He was probably in his thirties, but appeared older, his face almost cadaverous, his eyes narrow and slanting, and his thin black hair oiled and skimmed back tight against his scalp. He was neatly attired in a high-collared brown uniform with scarlet flashes of rank. He was scrawling on a parchment with a quill pen and when he looked up his eyes gleamed with amused malice.

'Sister Angostina, how pleasant to see you again so soon. What can be troubling you?'

'You know what is troubling me, Captain Romero. And I wish you would not call me sister. I no longer belong to a religious order.'

'But, of course, you abandoned your vows,' he smiled. 'How sensible of you. But, no, how should I know what is troubling you? As you see, I have so many affairs of this dreary little town to attend to, people wanting this, people wanting that. Do they never cease with their demands? Why me? Why am I posted to such a backward province? Am I being punished?'

'I know nothing of that, *jefe*, but I

might ask the same question: why are *we* being punished? Two weeks ago you promised that you would look into why the funds for the orphanage have not arrived, that we would have nothing to worry about. And there is still nothing. How can the nuns — I mean, the ladies at the orphanage who do the cooking, the washing, the shopping, how can they buy food? The children are practically starving. You have got to do something for us soon.'

'Got to?' Romero sat back in his big chair and stroked the quill pen against his cheek as he studied the young woman standing before him. 'Who are you, my dear, to tell me what I have got to do?'

'I am the official representative of the orphanage and President Juarez, himself, promised me that these funds would be provided. It is not much, for goodness sake, but to us it is everything.'

'You have plenty of buck, I'll give you that, Angostina.' He gave a thin-lipped smile but his eyes gleamed with lechery as he rose to his feet, placed his knuckles on the table and stared into her blue eyes that flashed defiance. 'I like that in a woman.'

'I'm not afraid of you, if that's what you mean,' she said, but trembled inwardly as she watched him march around the table towards her, his boots stomping on the stone flags.

Romero strode to the door and turned the big key. Angostina jumped, startled, as she heard the ominous sound. His footsteps returned until he was standing close beside her, his hands clasped behind his back. 'You are an exquisite-looking young woman, Angostina,' he whispered. 'You have abandoned your vows. That includes the vow of chastity, does it not? How old are you, twenty? That is old in Mexico for a girl to be still a virgin. Don't you think your time is due? I have told you I can help you, Angostina. I can take immediate action to see that your claim goes to the top of my list above all the others. You know how I can help you, don't you?'

'How can you be so corrupt? Haven't you been sent here to help these people? Isn't that what your revolution is all about? Have you no honour?' She did not face him but stood rigidly where she had been looking towards his desk. Suddenly she felt his tongue lick up her cheek and she recoiled.

Romero tittered and began to whisper more lascivious suggestions the like of which had never entered Angostina's sheltered mind before. 'It is so easy. All you have to do is slip out of your robes. Nobody will disturb us. Nobody will know. You can pray to your God at the same time, if you wish. And, lo and behold, tomorrow your money will arrive, your children will be fed.'

'You disgust me.' Angostina spun away from him as he tried to clutch at her hair. 'I hate you. You make my skin crawl. How can you be so foul?'

'Easily,' he smiled. 'It is your own fault for being so beautiful. Come on, sooner or later you've got to give in.'

'Leave me alone,' she screamed, as he followed her to the door. 'Let me out of here.'

He caught her hand as it closed over the key and his eyes were deadly cold as he stared into hers. 'Don't you realize I could have you shot?'

'Do your worst. Just let me go. I can't stand you.'

Arsenio Romero laughed, arrogantly. 'I give you three days to make up your mind. I will come to the convent. You will receive me in the mother superior's bedchamber. You will have everything prepared for an evening of pleasure.' He gripped her arm fiercely. 'Angostina, don't you understand? I *need* you.'

'Well, I don't need you. I'll get the money if I have to beg in the streets, if I have to go to Mexico City to see the president.'

'Don't be ridiculous,' he smiled. 'Expect me on Tuesday at seven in the evening. You will do this, Angostina, and you will do it willingly and I will become your protector. You will want for nothing.'

The girl swallowed her anger, shook her head, but did not reply as he unlocked the door for her. Her wide eyes met his, reproachfully, as he whispered, 'Go now. I will see you on Tuesday.'

'Oh, my God!' she implored, as she emerged onto the steps of the building and saw the town church, now hung with revolutionary banners. 'What am I going to do? Must I sacrifice myself?'

6

'I thought Texas was the hottest place on earth,' Seth Swanger growled as he splashed water from his canteen on his bandanna and wiped his enormous neck. 'But this beats everythang. I feel like I been boiled in cabbage leaves.'

Swanger's faded pink flannel under-vest was clinging to the bulges of his chest and belly, soaked with sweat. 'Look at that damn eagle up there. He's watchin' us, speculatin' whether we gonna make it through this desert or die.'

'Aw, quit bitchin',' James Slaughter replied. 'Nobody *asked* you to come along. And go easy on that water.'

The heat was, indeed, uncannily intense, like a heavy blanket pressing down on them. The air was so still, so hot, it was difficult to gulp it down into the lungs. The horses were sweating more than he cared to see, chomping on their bits, forequarters flecked with foam. He had called a halt to rest them and now they had their heads down in a dejected way vainly seeking something juicy to nibble among the thorns. Listlessly, they shook their manes and tails trying to toss away from their eyes the tormenting flies. Slaughter removed his leather hat and wiped his own sweat-plastered hair from his brow. He squinted up at the eagle lazily spiralling on the thermals, and beyond it to where the copper skein of cloud hanging over the ridge had turned into a dark viridescent hammerhead.

'It's that cloud that bothers me. It's movin' fast 'crost that hill an' it's comin' this way.'

'Aw.' Abel Funt sliced a piece of black tobacco and stuffed it in his mouth. 'If thass all that bothers you you're a lucky man.'

Slaughter glanced around them for possible shelter and noted a forest of tall saguaro cactii climbing up a ravine, their arms at jutted angles as if they were pleading for rain. In fact, they had gallons of water stored inside their prickly bodies. They knew how to survive. So did the ground squirrel who used his tail as a fan in the heat. And the desert rat who had learned how to burrow a staircase up through the saguaro limbs to reach the juicy fruit at the top. Slaughter, too, was beginning to feel the sapping effects of the heat pall.

Suddenly, a growl of thunder shook the earth and a hot, dry breeze struck them, swirling dust into their eyes, making the horses jump and snicker, nervously.

'Boys,' he cried, pointing to the black cloud heading their way, 'we better move up into them soo-aros an' fast. It's *El Viente de Diablo*. Thass what it is.'

'We'll ride it out,' Swanger snarled, irritably. 'I ain't stoppin' for no damn wind.'

But his beady eyes registered alarm and then fear as he saw that the hammer-head cloud was heading towards them, its tails trailing the ground. The wind preceding it had got stronger, slapping into them, rippling their hair, hatbrims and clothes. And the cloud had become a vast blue-black wall, travelling fast, blotting out the sun, churning up everything in its path.

'Hey, wait fer me,' he yelled and followed the others up into the ravine.

Slaughter jumped down, shouting, 'Get the horses in behind the cactus. Wrap your blankets over their eyes. Make 'em lie down.'

His black mustang had been trained for such an emergency, docilely lying down in the sand, but he had to use all his strength on the pack horse carrying their water keg, putting his arms around its neck, struggling to twist it onto its side. When it was finally down beside the other horse he wound his coat and his blanket about their heads and slumped on top of them, cruciform, holding them both.

He stared with horror at the great cloud like a tidal wave crashing towards them, dust devils spinning before it, tongues of blackness hanging down, licking at the earth like flails, cutting up bushes, chopping through the rocks. 'Get yourselves down.'

Suddenly the storm hit, lashing through the saguaro, peppering the air with a hail of stones and thorns, making a banshee screech that became a roar when it was all about them.

Slaughter stuck his head down between the horses' heads, hanging desperately on to them as a demonic, screaming force attempted to lift him and drag him away. He felt as if his clothes were being torn from his body, his teeth from his jaws, his hair from his skull. On and on the wind roared, unceasing, until he had lost track of time, knowing only a sense of oblivion, wondering how much longer he could hold the horses down, not let them all be swept away.

And then, as suddenly, it passed, rushing on, and the sun, at its zenith, reappeared and all was strangely still and silent. Slaughter slowly released his hold of the horses and looked about him. Behind him Abel and Swanger were prostrate across their mustangs, almost buried in the sand. When they moved and tried to struggle to their feet they looked like corpses rising from the grave.

'Holy Moses!' Swanger wiped dirt from his eyes and mouth. 'You were right, Loo-tenant. That was some Devil Wind.'

'Yeah.' Slaughter got to his feet, trying to brush himself down. 'I've heard of a man being caught out in it found dead, almost stripped to the bone.'

The men laughed with relief, getting themselves in order, blowing sand from the cylinders of their guns, mounting up and heading on. At least, the air was cooler now.

'Look at them giant soo-aros,' Swanger yelled. 'They been ripped in half.'

'Ridin' with you is makin' me jittery, Loo-tenant,' Abel Funt whined. 'What else we gonna meet?'

'Wall, I guess y'all be lucky ye ain't put up against a wall an' shot. Thass all I can promise you, boys.'

'Ain't that wind some sorta prelude to the rains?' Swanger called. 'Where they gotten to? It's September, ain't it?'

'How the hell should I know?' The sky was clear blue again. 'Maybe you better pray for it like the Injins do.'

'I thought you knew everythang, Loo-tenant.'

'If the rains come you'll be bitchin' 'bout that, too. Just shut up, you fat crab-louse.'

And, in such a spirit of harmony, they rode on their way . . .

★ ★ ★

'*Madre de Dios!*' Ygenio Guttierez pointed to the cloud of turkey vultures flapping and squabbling over the remains of the dead Mexicans in the ravine. 'There's been a massacre here.'

'Go take a look.' Dona Andrea sat her horse astride in her wide, split leather riding skirt, her hard face beneath the stiff-brimmed hat showing no sign of revulsion as the vultures, their pink heads daubed red with blood, dipped their beaks into human flesh, even though she did not care to get too near the fly-seething corpses herself. 'So that's what the shooting was about.'

They had heard the sound of battle echoing through the hills from miles distant for they were well behind the *Americano*, or he was well ahead for he was setting a fast pace. She watched the young, fancily attired hired-gun hopping about among the rocks clutching his bandanna to his mouth.

Jake Scullock leaned forward on his saddle horn and pointed to a black cloud seething across the ground some miles distant. 'We're lucky that missed us. Wonder iffen he got caught in it?'

'I hope so,' Raoul Yerby leered, revealing the gaps of his missing teeth. 'I hope it tore the flesh from his body.'

'Fifteen dead, all shot down,' Ygenio called as he ran back. 'One up on the ridge must have been making a break. Hoofprints up there of four other horsemen as if they were riding out in a hurry.'

'Holy Maria! Fifteen!' Raoul echoed. 'Who is he, this man? How can one man kill fifteen?'

'Maybe he'd got company?' Scullock pointed to other tracks in the sand of three or four horsemen moving out of the ravine. 'Maybe he ain't on his own no more? That would explain it.'

'Did you find any guns?' Dona Andrea snapped.

'No. *Nada*.'

'Damnation.'

She and her men were poorly armed. All they had been able to buy in Modero were some ill-made Confederate-issue arms, a Smith carbine that used rubber bullets, a single-shot Gallagher that broke at the breech for the insertion of a linen cartridge, a French Lefancheux .45 revolver, and a Griswold and Gunnison six-shooter that had been made with a brass frame due to iron shortages. Raoul toted a muzzle-loading Springfield rifle. Such creaky war souvenirs wouldn't be any match against three expert gunmen armed with repeating weapons. And to have killed fifteen *viciosos* these men must be experts.

Dona Andrea lashed her grey with her wrist quirt and spurred away. 'Whoever these men are,' she called to Scullock, as he rode up beside her, 'all the more reason to bide our time.'

On their spirited mounts the four pursuers loped along following the trail of prints for several hours until they spied the caravan of Mexican pedlars approaching and hauled in, greeting them. 'Have you seen any *gringos* riding this way?' Dona Andrea demanded.

The grizzled *zacatero* sat his mule and his face creased into a crafty smile. 'We may have or we may not have, that depends.'

'What are you talking about, man?'

'I mean that information, like water, is precious in this land, *señora*. What would you be willing to pay?'

Andrea regarded the ragged women and children in the team and raised her whip, threateningly. 'I will pay you with this for your insolence.'

'Wait a minute,' Scullock muttered, noting that several of the muleteers were packing pistols. 'We ain't well enough armed for trouble. Give him a couple pesos.'

Normally Andrea would have taken what she needed from such scum of the earth and, if they resisted, had them flogged or shot, but she realized that if it came to a fight they might be at a disadvantage. 'You're right, Jake. Very well,' she said, fishing out a silver peso from the loose bag on her hip. 'How much does this buy?'

The *zacatero* reached to take it, tested it in his teeth. 'Four more like this will make my tongue wag more readily.'

'Never.' She produced one more peso. 'This is all you get. It is outrageous. Now, speak.'

'Three *Americanos*. One big fat man. One skinny little man. And one medium-size, moustache, long black hair. He looked dangerous. But they are *loco*. Crazy men. They sell us all these horses for one barrel of water.'

Dona Andrea jagged back her lips in a grimace of agitation remembering the bounty-hunter's muscled body, the way he made love to her in Don Arturo's bed, his lithe, catlike grace. 'He is not so crazy. Life is more important than horses, isn't it? What a pity I didn't bribe him to work for me,' she whispered, more to herself, 'instead of these fools I ride with. We would have made a good team.'

'Isn't that information worth more than two pesos?' the *zacatero* wheedled. 'I know where they are headed.'

'So do we. Be grateful for small mercies. Be on your way and be thankful we let you go.'

The ragged processions stared sullenly at the imperious lady rider as she wheeled her mount and led her men towards the south.

The *zacatero* crossed himself and hissed, 'She has been kissed by the devil, that one.'

7

It had been a hard, long ride, his thighs ached and he was saddle sore, weary, dirty and sweat-stained, but as they came out of the pines on the shoulder of the mountain the ride was worth it just to see the city of Durango nestled on the plain below the towering Sierra Madre, the remembered city of jumbled houses with their tiled roofs, and the towers of massive stone churches rising above them, raised by the Conquistadors, or, more accurately, by their Indian slaves. He sat his mustang and took in the *mélange* of tawny walls and arches, amid the greenery of town parks and tree-lined streets. But it was also a busy town, stirring like a nest of ants; people, horses and wagons going back and forth, for it was one of the main mining centres of Mexico. Forget the old image of indolent Mexicans: they could work as hard as anybody if there was honest cash to be made and they could afford to put food in their bellies to give them the energy to work.

'Ole!' Slaughter shouted. 'Boys, we've arrived. Meet the city that never sleeps. The mines are working round the clock. The bars and whorehouses never close.'

'Thass what I like to hear,' Swanger beamed. 'Lead on. Is this where we find our crock of gold?'

'Maybe. Maybe not. It ain't gold; it's seams of silver running beneath those hills. but most of that's played out. You see that big mountain shaped like a flat iron beyond the city — the *Cerro del Mercado* — those chimney stacks pumping yellow smoke? It's iron ore they're mostly digging for these days.'

'Iron ore?' Abel Funt yelped. 'What good is that to us? We ain't come all this way to dig for iron, have we?'

Seth Swanger tapped a forefinger to his temple and raised his eyebrows at Slaughter. 'I told ya he ain't got all his slugs in his cylinder. No, dim brain, we ain't digging fer iron. If I know Slaughter he's got somethang else up his sleeve.'

'Like what?'

'Like we'll jest have to wait and find out, because you know the loo-tenant, he's kinda non-committal. But, he's gonna see us all right if we back his play, ain't that so, Loo-tenant?'

'Maybe.' Slaughter nudged his mustang down the slope towards the town. 'First thang I need is a bottle and a bath.'

'Me, too,' Swanger roared. 'In that order, or both at the same time.'

'An' a woman,' Abel squeaked. 'Thass my first priority. I can do without the tub. Anyway, I had one last year.'

'You dirty li'l runt,' Swanger shouted. 'It's us who has to put up with your gamey, rank stink. Why you think I allus bed-down upwind? You'll have a scrub in a tub an' like it.'

'Aw,' Abel sulked, 'that ain't fair.'

'Mark my words, you'll do better with the ladies if you whiff of French parfoom, not horse manure. An' you could do with a new suit. You've had that un on since the seige of Corinth, ain't ya?'

'What's wrong with it?' Abel protested, tugging at his soiled homespun. 'There's ten years' wear in this yet. I ain't wasting my cash — anyhow, I got business to attend to. I gotta go sell these guns.'

'Don't you two ever shut up?' James Slaughter shouted, sighing to himself.

He was undecided what to do first, whether to try to find Don Arturo's daughter, or try to find the hidden silver. Yes, like they said, he had to get his priorities right. First a bath and a bottle, then the silver. The daughter could wait a while. But, how, he wondered, as he jogged along beneath a vast cliff face pocked like Swiss cheese with the holes of mine entrances, most defunct, but some still being worked, was he to find the one where Don

Arturo had his his treasure? And, was it feasible that it would still be there? Had he come all this way on some fool's errand, on the say-so of some crazy old man?'

'Hey,' Swanger grinned, as they rode into the bustling city, 'the streets is paved. That's a novelty.'

'Yeah,' Abel hooted, 'but not with gold, only cobbles.'

As they clattered their way through the market stalls and food vendors, the wagons loaded with pit props and barrels, their horses' iron shoes hitting sparks off the stones, Slaughter said, 'It ain't so much a novelty. These paved streets and houses been here since the 1500s, before the States was even thought of.'

'Thanks for the history lesson, professor.' Swanger spotted a likely saloon, colourfully called, Creator of Illusions. Next door was a dentist's with the sign of a big, bloody tooth, and beside that a barber's and bathhouse. 'Everythang we need,' he said.

'Yeah.' Abel slid to the ground beside his worn-out plug. 'As long as they got some gals.'

'You got a one-track mind.' Swanger swaggered into the low-down, ill-lit dive, his carbine slung over his shoulder. 'What we gonna have? Tequila?'

Slaughter let them lead the way, his narrowed eyes getting used to the gloom, his Winchester crooked under one arm as he pulled off his torn leather gloves. He stood by a makeshift bar and glanced around. 'Waal, one thang's fer sure, the clientele's about as unsavoury looking as us.'

He filled a tumbler from a bottle of tequila, took a sip, and gave a braying, hawking laugh. And the more he laughed, the harder it was to stop. Soon his brays sounded more like a mule's as he doubled up.

'What's the matter with him?' Abel asked.

'Beats me,' Swanger beamed, punching Slaughter's shoulder and beginning to laugh, too. 'Guess there must be somethin' funny about this place.'

Slaughter calmed down, wiping the tears from his eyes, taking a bite of sliced lemon and a lick of salt. 'It's you two idjits, thass what's funny. I was just thinkin' as I rode in: they've followed me all this way, fer what? Fer nuthin'. I got a feelin' I'm on a wild goose chase.'

'Ah, don't listen to him,' Swanger grinned. 'He's just trying to put us off the scent.'

'No, it's true, fellas. I got the feelin' there ain't gonna be nuthin' at the end of this partic'lar rainbow.'

'But, you said — ' Abel Funt began.

'Arr, shuddup,' Swanger shouted, raising his liquor. 'There'll be some-thang. We gotta stick close to this lousy double-crosser, thass what we got to do.'

★ ★ ★

It was a riotous night. The steam bath wouldn't have been so bad if the ladies who ran it hadn't insisted on beating them with maize sticks — they said it was good for the circulation. The *pulque*, a kind of beer, they were served in half-gourds would have been palatable if Slaughter hadn't described how it was siphoned off the maguey plant, but most of it was human spit. The pile of black beans and chicken, mixed with squashed tomatoes, garlic and red hot chillis, served to them, might have been appetizing if the chef hadn't left the claws on the drumsticks. They stuck up like four scaly hands pleading for mercy. Or, perhaps, the *aquardiente* they had gone on to had made them a tad queasy on top of the pomegranate, mango, candied fruit and cream?

It had also made Abel Funt belligerent as he counted the cash from the sale of the guns. 'I ain't givin' you jerks none. You said not to bring 'em.'

'Don't call me a jerk,' Swanger hollered, grabbing at the pile of pesos. 'We're pards. We share and share alike.'

'You ain't no pard of mine.' Abel pulled out his hunting knife. 'You fat thief. I'll cut out your lights an' feed 'em to the dogs.'

Swanger caught his arm and throttled him, hoisting him from the floor. 'Calm down, boys,' Slaughter shouted, dragging them apart. 'It ain't worth shedding blood over.'

'No, you shouldn't quarrel.' Swanger soothed the coughing Abel, but slipped most of the pesos in his pocket. 'Not with me. I'm too strong for ya. Anyway, you owe me this. Here.' He pressed two pesos into Abel's hand. 'Go git yourself a woman. That'll git ya the best in town.'

'But there ain't none in here,' Abel whined.

'So, let's go look fer some,' Swanger shouted, holding on to Abel unsteadily as he weaved him towards the door.

They were back in the heady throng of the street again, pushing past beggars, miners dragging overloaded pack jacks, Indian women crouched down on their mats with a few pathetically gnarled fruit to sell, wagons crunching by, a wandering band of musicians blasting out discordant music on drums, trumpets and guitars for a few *centavos*, innumerable stalls selling hot snacks, cakes or sweet rolls, roasted squash, *tortillas* stuffed with eggs, onions, or purple meat of debatable source, the aroma of frying oil mingling with the ripe brew of horse droppings and ever-prevalent human sewage that had failed to wash away in these days of drought.

'Ah, the stench of Mexican humanity,' Slaughter shouted, his arms hanging around his *compadres'* shoulders. 'It passeth understanding.'

Past a *curandera*'s booth offering hundreds of instant cures from an alligator's tooth to calm the pangs of love, an ants' nest to be eaten boiled for hiccoughs, nausea or bronchitis, or, most expensive and popular of all, crushed human coccyx to give an instant erection. 'I'll try some of that,' Abel cried.

Seth Swanger was more taken by a

big Negro who stood swaying and smiling, eight cigarillos of marijuana stuffed between his outstretched fingers and thumbs. 'If it puts him in happy land it cain't be so bad,' he grinned, taking two thick sticks for two pesos.

'You durn fool,' Abel warned. 'Everyone knows that stuff induces madness that often ends in murder. And it's illegal.

'Waal, if it's illegal it must be good for ya.' Swanger grinned, benevolently, and pushed through a bead curtain into a *pulqueria* named The Parted Lips. 'This looks more like our kinda place.'

From what Slaughter could make out in his semi-inebriated state through the fug of cigar fumes and Swanger's sweet-scented baccy it was a dance-hall-cum-gambling den. A band on the stage was wailing and strumming some love lament as a Latin Romeo, a skimpily clad girl in his arms, strutted back and forth in an erotic dance, or so they thought. The male, with brillian-tined curls, ruffed shirt and pants fitting tight as gloves was singing, 'Cooling to my thirst is your fresh mouth on mine . . . ' while the girl just clung to him as if glued.

'Hey, get an eyeful of her,' Abel Funt leered, as he sprawled on a stool and called for mescal, the most evil drink of all.

As if from nowhere two women had appeared, one large with ponderous breasts restrained by a floppy, flowered dress, the other skinny as a lath, both with savage Indian faces and black hair. Blotchy lavender powder and scarlet rouge hadn't much helped hide nature's defects. They squeezed into the booth with the boys, fixed smiles on their faces.

'Whay-hay!' Swanger, dopily bemused by the reefer in his lips, drawled, 'Who whistled up these two dawgs?'

'Hey, they're the best, man,' Abel giggled. 'The darker and dirtier the better, say I. We gonna have some fun.'

'Two's company, three's a crowd,' Slaughter muttered, sidling out of the women's clutches.

'Hey, where you goin'?' Swanger tried to snatch at his sleeve.

'There's the dang hosses to be fed,' he said, pulling away. 'Don't you two ever think of that? I'll go bed 'em down in the livery. See you boys at the Illusions. I'll book us a room.'

★ ★ ★

He left them in their besotted and befuddled state and wandered back to attend to the broncs. He hadn't drunk too much after the tequila and was reasonably clear-headed apart from a kind of roll to his gait that made him feel like he was on a ship in a storm. He steadied himself against the hitching rail and led the horses around to a high-gated livery they had passed.

'Howdy,' he greeted the blacksmith. 'Can you give 'em a feed and some straw in a stall? And the back left shoe on my black looks like it needs fixing. OK?'

'Sure, *señor*. You come far?'

'Quite a way. I'm lookin' for an old guy called Rodrigo Cruz. He used to be a foreman to one of the big mines. You heard of him?'

'No.' The blacksmith shook his head as he pulled the mustang's hoof up between his thighs and began to prise out the nails of the shoe. 'Try in the *cantinas*, somebody will have heard of him. Durango isn't such a big place.'

Slaughter stuck a bill in his pocket and strolled out into the night. The trouble was how many saloons and *cantinas* were there in this place, about fifty at a rough guess? And that was only in the centre of town.

He started in the Flower of the Desert and proceeded to other ornately named drinking dens, The Gate of Hell, The Deluge, The Tower of Babel, and The Golden Girl to name a few, their walls gaudily decorated to illustrate the theme, but his question resulted in similar negative shakes of the head, or suggestions to try elsewhere. Some had heard of Cruz from fifteen years or so before, but had no idea where he might be.

About midnight, he sipped yet another murky, milky mug of *pulque* in another *pulqueria* and watched a crude striptease on stage as an embarrassed Indian girl shed her clothes amid jeers and catcalls, and asked his question of the bartender.

'*Si*,' he shouted above the din, jerking his thumb. 'He lives around the corner in Calle Domingo. The end house, I think.'

Slaughter hammered on a wooden door of one of a row of houses more like stables and an old man with grey, grizzled hair and beard, his face as dark as mahogany, stuck out his head.

'What do you want here?'

'Rodrigo? Rodrigo Cruz?'

'*Si*, that's me. What of it?'

'Don Arturo sent me.'

'Don Arturo? Who's he?'

'Don Arturo del Briganza de Apuarte. You were foreman of his mine for

122

twenty-seven years.'

'Not me, mister. You got the wrong man. I don' know what you talk about.' Rodrigo eyed the muscular, black-haired *hombre* in his worn leather coat and at the same time Slaughter noticed the pinned-back sleeve of the old man's shirt. 'Why don't you go away and let me sleep?'

'Before the accident. Don Arturo figures you deserve some recompense.'

'Yes, I lost my arm when a mine caved in, but I have never heard of this Don Arturo whatever you call him.'

'It's OK. I'm a friend. How about Ecclesiastes, Chapter Six? How's it go? There is an evil which I have seen under the sun and it is common among men . . .'

Rodrigo glanced around but the street was deserted. 'There are a lot of evil men around, *señor*. You had better come in.'

Inside was not much different to most Mexican hovels. No such thing as furniture. A pile of rags to serve as a bed. A straw mat. A charcoal cooking fire. A few cracked pots. Some bits of food wrapped in newspaper. The only light came from a candle flickering in front of a carved saint set back in the wall.

'You want a drink?' Rodrigo asked, pointing to a gourd.

'No. I've had my fill looking for you.'

'How is Don Arturo?'

'Not so good. You know a woman who calls herself Dona Andrea?'

'Andrea? Did she marry him?'

'Nope. I guess she's given herself the title Dona. She is holding him captive. She and three gunmen — a couple of Mexican boys and some two-bit, four-flushing Texan.'

'Texan?'

'Yeah, I might be Texan, too, but I ain't no four-flusher. Not yet.'

'Floor-flusher? You mean he washes floors?'

'No. Never mind. He's just some regular badhat. The bad news is I figure they're following me.'

'Here? In Durango? I don' wan' trouble, señor.'

Slaughter glanced around. 'You want to live like this the rest of your life?'

'It is good enough. My needs are few, señor.'

'Don Arturo told me to give you ten thousand pesos in silver if you show us where his cache is. He says it is time to reclaim his nest egg. I am to give a quarter to his wife and a quarter to his daughter. Like I say, ten thousand of his share to go to you.'

'No.' Rodrigo shook his head in a hang-dog way. 'Andrea and her gunmen will want the silver, too. She will kill anyone who gets in the way. You had better go, mister. I don't want to know about this.'

'Come on, where's your spirit, man?' Slaughter patted his Schofield. 'Don't worry, I will protect you.'

'No.' Again the old man shook his head and stared at the floor. 'This can only end badly. I have only a few years left, but I do not want to die just yet.'

'Just think, you will be able to live in comfort, as much food and wine as you need. Why, you could even buy yourself a woman.'

'No thank you, that I don't need,' Rodrigo grinned. 'Anyhow, you could never get in there. There was a big fall. The mine was sealed off.'

'Don Arturo seemed pretty confident you could find a way in.'

Slaughter squatted cross-legged and fished out a couple of cheap cheroots from his pocket. They were silent for a while as they lit up. 'At least, draw me a map. Maybe I can find the place myself.'

'I do not need ten thousand pesos,' Rodrigo mused. 'It is too much. It would draw attention to me. Say six thousand, that will be enough.'

'You'll do it? Good man.' Slaughter offered his hand and shook. 'It's a deal. You think we can get in?'

'We can try, señor. We will need ropes, crowbars, helmets, lamps, gunpowder. It will not be easy.'

'Nuthin's easy that's worth having. We'll start first light.'

'Meet me at the Mount of Our Lady of Remedies. It is close by the Cerro del Mercado. You can't miss it. There is a white church with a tapering spire. I will wait there.'

'Right, as soon as we buy the stuff we'll be there. Or, I will. I'll try to give them other two monkeys the slip. That shouldn't be hard. They'll be hungover as hell.'

'Monkeys?'

'Aw, just two *gringos* who've attached themselves to me. I'll cut them in for a small share.' Slaughter got to his feet. 'I'd better get back and get some shut-eye. By the way, you any idea where I can find Don Arturo's wife and daughter?'

'His wife died many years ago. The daughter went to the nuns.'

'Our Lady of Guadeloupe convent? Where is that?'

'About fifteen miles out of Santa Julia on the shores of the lake. But the nuns fled. I do not know if Angostina would still be there.'

'Angostina? You knew her?'

'Yes, when she was a small girl.'

'Well, I guess she must be a big girl now. See you tomorrow, Rodrigo. Or should I say later this morning. Remember, I'm relying on you.'

'I have given my word. I will help you if I can.'

'Right. *Adios, amigo*. Don't be late.'

8

Slaughter awoke in the barnlike bedroom of the Creator of Illusions lying on the hard floor. He never did have much time for beds after being accustomed to sleeping out in the open for so long. Nor had he fancied joining Swanger and Funt in the creaky double they were ensconced in.

'Aw, Jessis!' Swanger sat up and began vigorously scratching at his middle parts. 'What the devil have I picked up? Musta got it from them hoo-ers.'

'No, I told you not to turn this filthy mattress,' Abel hollered, digging frenziedly at his own groin. 'You musta stirred up everythang in there that hops and crawls. Ooh, I cain't sit still.'

He hopped out of bed in his grimy drawers closely followed by Swanger. 'Boys,' Slaughter grinned, as he watched

129

them dance about the room. 'I reckon you got a bad dose of the crabs.'

'Oh, no,' Abel shrieked, sitting down and jumping up again. 'I cain't stand it. What we gonna do?'

'We better go see one of them *curanderas*,' Swanger moaned, peering into the dense foliage inside his pants. 'See if they got a cure.'

'It's excruciating,' Abel howled. 'We gotta do somethang.'

James Slaughter was shaving in cold water, peering into a little cracked mirror, scraping the razor across his stone-grey jaws.

He wiped his chin dry, found his brass telescope and said, 'Drop your pants. Let's take a peek.'

'There's one!' Abel Funt snatched at something between his fingernails, picking it from out of his pubic hair. 'Got it!' He dropped it on the canvas covered top of a rickety table. 'See, there! And another! And another!'

Slaughter studied the table-top through the telescope. 'Yeah,' he breathed. 'I got 'em. L'il varmints.' He watched a minute crab louse, magnified, scuttle away sideways across the table. 'Look at the pincers on that. I wouldn't like to have 'em clawing at me. They're just like real li'l white crabs. Yuk!'

'Yow!' Seth Swanger yelped. 'Look, I got one. There's one from me.'

'Yes, very nasty,' Slaughter muttered, putting the 'scope back in its leather case. 'There's only one remedy. You boys gotta shave yourselves with your cut-throats down there — an' make sure you don't cut nuthin' off — then go down to the corrals and get some of that *tecole* grease they daub on cows' ears when they've jingle-bobbed 'em to stop the maggots gettin' in. You gotta spread that all over your underparts. That should kill 'em.'

'Oh, Christ!' Swanger moaned. 'This is some job. Can I borrow some of your soap?'

'Sure.' Swanger stood up fully dressed, lighting a cheroot and pulling his hat over his thick black thatch.

131

'Help yourselves. Best of luck, boys. I'm gonna git me a cawfee.'

He laughed as he clambered down the *cantina*'s stairs. 'That should keep 'em busy for a while.'

* * *

'There he is,' Dona Andrea hissed, 'He's coming out of that mining store. He's bought himself a crowbar and a keg of gunpowder. Keep back. We don't want him to see us.'

'*Si*, and those other two, the large and the little one, they came out of the same hotel,' Ygenio said. 'They were jumping about like they had ants in their pants, heading down to the town corral. What's the matter with them?'

'Ha! All *gringos* are crazy. Didn't you know?' Raoul glanced at Scullock. 'With the exception of you, maybe.'

'I must be crazy to come along with you three,' Jake growled. 'Step back behind this stall or he'll see us. He's packing the stuff on his spare mustang.'

'What about the other two?'

'He's the one we've got to watch,' Andrea smiled. 'With any luck he's going to lead us straight to what we're looking for. Get ready to ride.'

★   ★   ★

Slaughter was two hours or so late for the appointment, but, this being Mexico, so was Rodrigo, who turned up on his moke, with pick and shovel roped behind, climbing up to the white church an hour later.

'Look,' he said, 'if you stand here and take a line up across the church steeple to a point on the side of the mountain that's where the old mine entrance used to be. It would take weeks to tunnel in there and you would need pit props and many labourers.'

'So?'

Cruz raked his toes in the dust. 'See, this is the mine entrance going fifty metres into the side. This is the shaft going down another fifty metres. As I

133

remember it there was a fault that ran through from the foot of the shaft to a point lower down the mountain. If we can find that crack we can start from there.'

'You gonna use gunpowder? Won't that cause a cave-in?'

'In mining there is always danger of a collapse. We must be careful.'

'Right. What are we waiting for? Let's get started.'

They climbed up through the rocks to the sheer mountainside, leading the animals. When Slaughter had unloaded the tools he looked around but Rodrigo was nowhere in sight. Suddenly he popped his head up out of the hole and called, 'I've found it. Come on, *Andale!*'

They roped themselves together and the American squeezed in after him. They lit carbide lamps on their helmets and by the light thrown in the pitch darkness eased up into a narrow crevice out of which a trickle of water flowed. Soon they were confronted by a perpendicular wall. 'You wait here,' the old man said. 'I'll go up and take a look.'

Slaughter watched his scrawny, bare, brown legs disappear up into a tiny hole that looked barely big enough for a snake to wriggle through, let alone a man. Small stones were dislodged and rained down on his head. But then the light disappeared and he was left in eerie silence, apart from the occasional creak of what sounded like rocks moving, which made his heart thump. Being entombed in the bowels of the earth by a rockfall wasn't exactly his idea of fun.

There was a theatrical whisper from up above. 'We're going to have to do some digging. Untie your rope and send the tools up.'

When this was done the rope snaked back down and Slaughter got a hold of it to haul himself up. 'I better leave my six-gun down here,' he called. 'It's gonna git in the way.' His words echoed up to the unseen man and he began to climb. It was more than a tight fit getting through the hole and for awful moments he thought he was stuck.

Rodrigo caught one of his hands and pulled him up through. 'There's been a fall. The way is blocked. We've got to go on upwards at almost ninety degrees.' He took a cord with a stone attached from his pocket and held it up as a plumbline. 'Yes, I don't think we're far off course. I can't do much digging with one arm, so, *muchacho*, it's up to you. Start hacking through that rubble.'

Sweat began to pour from Slaughter as he hammered and hacked with the crowbar at the roof of rock blocking their way. He tore his shirt off, his body glistening in the lamplight as he went at it harder. There was a sudden shower of rock and a boulder tumbled down upon them. Slaughter jumped back, expecting the worst. But the fall eased and he could see the possibility of a passageway. He took the pick and began swinging it as hard as he could in the restricted space.

'Careful,' Rodrigo cautioned. 'Not so hard. Use the crowbar as a probe. We don't want the whole lot coming down on us.' He crossed himself and tried to hold the lamp at a better angle. 'Up there, see?'

'Yeah,' Slaughter grunted, spitting on his palms and starting again. 'Maybe if I just wiggle the crowbar up through here. I sure wish I hadn't had all that *pulque* last night.'

He jammed his feet against the rock walls gradually working his way higher, his legs and body aching with the strain of holding him poised fighting gravity and with hacking at the dirt blocking his way. Suddenly it felt as if the crowbar had hit a sandbag. He groped at the sacking with his hand and tore it apart.

'Jeesis!' he shouted as a stream of silver pesos suddenly poured down onto his hand, plus heavier gold coins bearing the Austrian double-headed eagle. 'It's raining cash up here.'

His face split into a grin as the silver

and gold slithered over him and down onto Rodrigo below. 'Watch out,' he called as he got hold of the tightly packed gunny sack and hurled it down. 'Don't wanna kill ya with cash.'

He wiped the dust from his eyes and spat to clear his throat. 'I'm going on up through.' He climbed out into a small chamber where there were signs of mining, an iron tub, a pair of discarded boots, candle stubs and a broken pick. There were four other bulging sacks. He carefully opened one and put in his hand. He came out with a slim bar of silver. There were a good thirty more inside. 'Rodrigo,' he called, his voice hushed with awe. 'We've hit the jackpot. This must be it.'

'Good. I was dreading the prospect of having to blast our way through with gunpowder.'

'Me, too. We've done it, pal. You were right on target.'

'Take a good look around. See if there's any more.'

Slaughter stepped carefully along a

low-roofed tunnel. Suddenly he jerked back with horror as he saw a grinning human skull, the clawing arm of a skeleton protruding from what must have been a rockfall. 'Eugh! The poor devil. He musta been trapped alive.'

He retraced his steps and called, 'There's just four sacks of silver ingots. I'll lower 'em down.'

When he had done this he slithered down to rejoin Rodrigo. 'There's some poor miner up there, trapped from the waist down. He ain't a pretty sight. It gave me quite a turn, I gotta admit.'

'Yes, one man was missing at the time. Don Arturo decided we would never have got to him in time through such a huge fall.'

'Don Arturo wouldn't have caused that fall, himself, in order to seal off his treasure?'

Rodrigo Cruz's eyes swivelled, guiltily, in the darkness. 'How would I know? I got caught in the fall at the other end, myself. I had to have my arm amputated and nearly died from loss of blood and shock to the system.'

'But surely you would have remembered, if there was an explosion?'

'No . . . I can't say . . . there might have been . . . in the adjacent tunnel,' Rodrigo replied, hesitantly. 'Men were always blasting. It was common practice. They were crazy.'

'You wouldn't have stayed quiet?' Slaughter drawled, studying the old man. 'To protect Don Arturo?'

'No. Why should I? I was finished. Old before my time. It is true he gave me a small pension and begged me never to speak of the silver he had hidden. This' — he shrugged and opened his palms towards the treasure — 'this was all his. He was the mine-owner. Why should I want to steal from him? So I said nothing until you came along. You knew his line from Ecclesiastes so I knew I could trust you.'

'Right.' Slaughter offered him his hand and smiled. 'Well, we've done it, old-timer. Now we'd better git this loot out.'

'*Si*.' Rodrigo grinned for the first time since they had met. 'It was certainly much easier to find than I feared.'

'Yeah, maybe too easy. Maybe we'd better not count our chickens just yet.'

But, when they finally got the coins and silver down to the slit in the side of the hill, saw the gleam of sunlight, and clambered out, count it, they did.

Rodrigo raised his hands to the blue sky and cried out, 'Look at God's glorious heaven. Listen to that bird singing. Isn't that more precious than any gold or silver?'

'It sure is. It's great to be back out in the open air. But, a bit of silver in the pocket can make the world seem even more remarkable.'

The hillside appeared to be deserted and it was still only mid-afternoon so Slaughter knelt down and did his sums. 'At a rough count I'd say there's sixty-thousand pesos worth of silver in each of these four sacks. And, those Austrian coins are solid gold, so maybe they're worth another fifty thousand. What say you?'

'Yes, that's about my estimate, too.'

'Waal, seeing as Don Arturo's wife is dead she won't be needin' hers, so I think the fairest way would be to divide this lot into three portions, one to go to his daughter, one to me, and you can take what you think is your fair share from Arturo's third.'

'But, *señor*, shouldn't the lady's quarter now go to her daughter?'

'Aw, what does some convent gal want with all that loot?' Slaughter gave a conning grin. 'I told Arturo I don't come cheap. It's you and me who've taken the risk and done the hard work. Personally, I think you should take as much as you wish, Rodrigo. Go on, think big. Celebrate.'

'No, I said six thousand pesos would be enough. That will do for me.' Rodrigo opened a canvas sack and began counting the silver bars. 'Each of these bars must be worth two thousand pesos. So, I will take three of them. OK, *amigo*?'

'Thass OK by me, my friend. Help yourself. And *muchas gracias*.'

'*Si, muchas gracias*,' a woman's voice rang out as Dona Andrea stepped out from behind a rock, the .45 Lefancheux in her hand and aimed at Slaughter's chest. 'It is very kind of you, *señors*.'

The bounty hunter sprang to his feet, his right hand streaking towards the Texan Schofield in the gunbelt he had hitched back on around the waist of his jeans.

'No,' Scullock growled, jabbing the barrel of his Griswold & Gunnison into Slaughter's bare spine. 'I wouldn't do that. Not unless you wanna be blasted to smithereens.'

'Waal,' Slaughter drawled, poised mid-act, stretching out his empty fingers. 'Ain't life a bitch?'

'It sure is, buddy.' Raoul Yerby gave his gappy grin and smashed the butt of his Smith carbine into Slaughter's abdomen, making him double-up and collapse onto one knee. He took his Schofield and tossed it into the rocks.

Young Ygenio, in his tight velveteens, caught the Texan by the hair and smiled, viciously. 'This is for the ones you gave me.' He smashed his fist into the bounty-hunter's jaw, spinning him in his tracks.

'*Señora* . . . *señors* . . . this is not right.'

Raoul turned to Rodrigo. 'Stay outa this, grandad, if you wanna stay alive.' He snatched up his canvas sack of silver as the old man tried to hang onto it, back-handed him hard across the jaw. Rodrigo went flying back from the blow and, as he fell, cracked his head hard against a rock. Blood began to flow from the side of his head as he groaned and lost consciousness.

Jake Scullock turned his six-shooter on him, aiming and cocking it, a scowl on his bearded face. 'You shoulda stayed outa this, old man.'

'No.' Andrea put out a hand to restrain him. 'Leave him. I think he's finished, anyway. We don't want to draw attention to ourselves.

'That's true,' Jake said, for they were well in earshot of copper miners passing backwards and forwards on the trail.

'So, what's wrong with a knife?' Raoul asked. 'Isn't that silent enough?'

'You may use it on the *gringo*, perhaps,' Dona Andrea replied. 'But first I have a question for him.'

Slaughter got to his feet, his black hair hanging over his face. 'What's that?'

'Why bother with Don Arturo? He is an old man. He is finished. You would do better to come with me. There is enough here for all of us.'

'Yeah, mebbe there is,' he drawled, huskily, his green eyes glimmering in their slits as he watched her. 'But once I give my word to work for a man, that's it. I have to go through to the bitter end.'

'Don't be a fool. I like you. I don't want to have you killed. We would be good together.' There was a note of pleading in the older woman's voice, in her dark eyes. 'You could have Don

Arturo's house, his lands. You could live like a rich *haciendado*. We both could.'

Still shirtless, Slaughter's fine-sculpted muscles flexed as he pushed Ygenio's threatening fist aside and he faced her, wide-chested, and flicked the hair from his eyes. 'Waal, ma'am, that's a mighty handsome offer and don't think I ain't grateful. And like I said to Don Arturo, you sure are mighty slick in the sack, but, I wonder, do I want to spend the rest of my life as some old lady's bed-warmer?'

'Are you gone crazy, Andrea?' Scullock roared. 'You're talking through your — '

'Shut up, Jake,' she snapped, and pleaded with the American, 'Who are you? What's your real name? Don't you understand, I don't want to use you? We would be equal partners. We would be married. We would be rich.'

'*You* shut up Andrea,' Scullock shouted, grabbing her arm and shaking her. 'You're making me sick. If you marry anybody it's gonna be me, not this sage rat.'

'You?' Andrea cried. 'Why should I want you?'

'Because it was me put the pressure on Don Arturo, made him sign the house and land over to you. Because we got a deal.'

'You?' Dona Andrea screamed, turning her .45 on Scullock. 'It's you who's crazy.' She fired point-blank into the middle-aged Texan's chest, and he tumbled back, blood flowering on his shirt. 'You dirty fool. Nobody owns me.'

Slaughter gave a low whistle of awe. 'You're a very insistent woman, aincha? If you put it like that maybe I might be advised to jine ya.'

Suddenly a bullet whined and ricocheted through the rocks cutting away Andrea's earlobe and she spun around. She had forgotten her own admonition not to give their position away. She screamed as she tried to staunch the blood and fired the ancient Lefancheux wildly at a puff of carbine smoke along in the rocks. Another rifle shot cracked out from close to the first one and this nearly took off her stiff-brimmed hat.

Raoul and Ygenio had crouched for cover, turning to fire at the attackers. Slaughter, unarmed, stayed poised on his toes, waiting his chance. But a bullet ploughed into Raoul's chest and he heard Swanger's booming laugh as he shouted, 'Thar's one for the pot!'

A look of consternation had spread over the handsome young features of Ygenio as he realized the marksmen's bullets were too close for comfort and his fat friend was writhing on the ground in his death throes, but still trying with futile greed to grasp the pack of silver ingots.

Slaughter took his chance and dived in, grabbing Ygenio's gun-wrist and slamming his fist into his face. But, as Ygenio reeled back, Abel showed himself, his rifle at his shoulder, and the slug thudded unerringly into Ygenio's back. The young Mexican screamed and shuddered as the bullet tore a hole right through him, and he fell on top of Raoul.

'*Basta!*' Dona Andrea screamed, and turned her revolver on Slaughter, firing twice. But, such was her haste to scramble away, both shots missed by narrow margins. She ran to her high-stepping grey, climbed into the saddle, and whipped him away.

Slaughter picked up Raoul's solid-frame Smith carbine, rested it on his forearm and took aim at her. 'Aw, hell,' he growled as he let her go. 'I ain't into shooting wimmin.'

He wiped Ygenio's blood from his chin — splashed over him when the bullet tore through the young man's body. Swanger and Funt had scrambled up to join him. 'I got a feelin' we'll be seein' some more of her,' Slaughter drawled. 'Thanks, boys, you saved my skin again.'

'Hey look at the silver conchos on this sombrero,' Abel whooped, picking up Ygenio's hat. 'And how about these silver-toed boots?'

'Fergit 'em, you bird-brained small-timer,' Swanger shouted, dipping into the sacks of silver. 'We're rich. This is worth a fortune.'

'Don't get any funny ideas, boys,' Slaughter said. 'The largest part of this goes to my client and his daughter.'

'You what, are you crazy, you dumb hick?' Abel hooted. 'To the victors the spoils. You can forget about them, whoever they are.' He wrested the packet of three silver bars from Raoul's death grip. 'Look at these.'

'Not so fast.' Slaughter took the ingots off him. 'That's the old man's share.'

He knelt down and tried without success to revive Rodrigo. He tore a strip from the old Mexican's shirt and tied it tight round his head to try to stop the bleeding. 'He's earned this and he happens to be my friend. I gotta git him to a medic.'

'Don't be a fool, man,' Swanger bellowed. 'It's us three now. Fair shares, a three-way split.'

'Oh, no.' The bounty hunter hauled Rodrigo up and slung him across his *burro.* 'Though I say so myself I got a reputation of being a man who sees a job through. And that's what I'm gonna do.'

'Come on, Loo-tenant,' Swanger wheedled. 'We just saved your worthless ass once again. You owe us a fair split.'

'We better git rid of these bodies.' Slaughter ignored them and slowly dragged Scullock, Ygenio and Raoul into the hole in the hillside, tossing their guns in after them, except for Raoul's carbine which he kept in his hands, prowling to take a stand with his back to the sun. 'You two got a grievance you're gonna have ta go through me. This ain't my usual piece so you got the advantage today.'

'Right,' Abel hollered. 'Thass what we'll do. You ready, Swanger? It's time we showed this jackanapes who's in charge.'

'Shut your fool mouth.' Swanger was well aware of the bounty-hunter's speed even without his Schofield with its filed-down hammer. He stroked his chin, nervously. 'We can talk about this.'

Abel Funt was too riled up to talk. He jerked his revolver from his belt and aimed at Slaughter, but, simultaneously, he must have been bitten by a crab louse for he cried, 'Ouch!' and scratched at his crotch. It put him off his aim. However, anticipating attack, Slaughter had determinedly replied, squeezing the trigger of the carbine. The bullet hit Abel in the chest knocking him back — running and tumbling against the rocks.

'Ouch!' he said again as he lay on his back, looked down at his chest for blood and found none. 'That hurt.'

Slaughter looked puzzled. 'What's in this thang?' He turned the cylinder and picked out a cartridge from the breech. 'Rubber bullets. Well, I'll be damned.' He cracked out laughing as he looked across at Swanger. 'How about you, Seth? You fancy one?'

'Fergit it,' Swanger growled. 'What on earth was he carrying rubber bullets around fer?' He went over and hauled Abel to his feet. 'You're lucky to be alive.'

'Aw.' Abel rubbed his chest and crotch simultaneously. 'If it weren't for these damn crabs I coulda kilt him.'

Slaughter contemplated them with a smile. 'Boys, I'm feeling generous. I'll tell ya what I'm gonna do. We'll split — a quarter to my client, Don Arturo, a quarter to his daughter, a quarter to yours truly, and the fourth quarter you two can split between you. That's my last offer.'

'That ain't fair,' Abel whined.

'It's the best you're gonna git.'

Swanger sighed with relief. If it came to another shoot-out the bounty hunter would get one if not both of them. He had seen him in action. 'All right,' he shouted. 'That sounds fine by me. It is your job, after all.'

'How much is our share?'

Slaughter shrugged at Abel. 'About seventy thousand pesos. Ain't it enough for you, you greedy li'l runt?'

'Uh — well — yeah.'

'So, let's get it loaded up. I'm taking Rodrigo back to town. You can come along. Or you can take your split and clear out.'

'Aw, we'll stick with you, Loo-tenant,' Swanger grinned, and muttered to Abel as they worked, 'We'll bide our time. We'll git more outa this, you'll see.'

'Yeah,' Abel snarled. 'Thang to do is jump him in the night.'

'Yeah, but we won't kill him, 'cause he did tell us about that *tecole* grease and most my bugs is gone.'

'Yeah? Well, mine ain't. And I gone all blue down there.'

'You're lucky it ain't dropped off.'

Slaughter had gone to look for his Texan Schofield in the rocks where it had been tossed by Raoul. He had had it a long time. It was like part of him. The first thing was to get Rodrigo back to his hut, find a woman to care for him, leave him his share of the silver. Then he would go look for Don Arturo's daughter.

As they climbed the horses back down to the trail by the church, a miner had stopped his wagon and called out, 'What was all that shooting about?'

'Aw, nuthin',' Slaughter said. 'Just a bit of target practice, thassall.'

9

Angostina was teaching the children their seven-times table in sing-song fashion — 'five sevens are thirty-five' — their voices fluted after hers in chorus. There were twenty of the older children, aged from six to ten. The younger ones were being tended by Sister Maria — no, she must remember, nowadays it was simply Maria.

Suddenly she heard the sound of horses' hooves and jingle of harness and, looking from the high narrow window, she saw a small column of soldiers approaching at a jog along the side of the lake. Her heart sank when she recognized at their head the thin, sallow face of Arsenio Romero. 'Oh, no,' she hissed.

She instructed the children to take up their slates and copy down some simple arithmetic lessons she chalked on the board. She was filled with dread as she heard a shouting and clattering as the Juaristas wheeled into the courtyard of the former convent. There was panic fluttering in her. Perhaps she could hide? Perhaps she could pretend to be sick? No, she knew it was no use. It seemed as if her fate was sealed.

She heard his boot-steps on the stone stairway and sensed him enter the schoolroom. 'What do you want?'

Arsenio Romero stood there in his neat uniform. 'You know what I want.'

'Have you brought our funds?'

'I have told you when you will get your funds.'

Angostina looked at the curious eyes of the children, their thin arms protruding from their blue smocks, their skinny legs and faces pinched with hunger. Her mouth was so dry she could hardly speak. 'The children have to have their supper, what little there is.'

'Don't keep me waiting too long. I will rest tonight in the chamber. Come to me there. That is an order, not a request.'

Angostina wanted to squeeze her head in her hands and scream, 'Why don't you leave me alone?'

But, again, a sense of desolation came over her. What could she do? The children had to eat. What was her honour worth beside that? What did her precious purity matter any more? She would not be the first to be sacrificed. She would have to go with this monstrous man and do this loathsome thing and pray that she did not have his child, pray for forgiveness from God, pray that Romero kept his word.

She took a deep breath and whispered, 'I understand. I will be there in an hour.'

He clicked his heels and departed down to the courtyard, no doubt, to see that his men were settled down and their horses fed. He would spruce himself up, smile at himself in his shaving mirror: oh, the sickening arrogance and piggishness of such vain and corrupt men! It crossed her mind to take a carving knife, kill him, then kill herself. But she knew she could not.

She dismissed the class and saw to the children's needs. 'The captain wants to see you,' Maria hissed. 'He is in the mother superior's room. He wants you to dine with him. He has brought the best of food and wine. Aren't you lucky?'

'Am I?' Would that she were luckier to be old and wrinkled like Maria.

The old nun looked at the girl fearfully as she prepared to leave. 'Be good to him, Angostina, for all our sakes.'

The girl did not reply, nor make any attempt to beautify herself apart from washing her hands and face and straightening her blonde hair, but she would have done that at all times. She had been taught to be clean and neat.

Angostina passed through the chapel which had once been an orgy of ornamentation with its saints and seraphims, but now, looted, its statuettes smashed, appeared dark and forlorn. The wooden statue of Christ still stood on its plinth by the dusty altar and Angostina knelt before it and crossed herself before climbing up the circular stone staircase to the chamber. She felt as if she was walking into the flames of Hell. She paused and steeled herself before knocking and entering.

Arsenio Romero greeted her with false joviality, attempting to kiss her hand, draw her near to him. Angostina remained coldly aloof but allowed herself to be seated at a table loaded with sweetmeats and delicacies. Romero had spared no expense to impress her.

'Have some turkey breast,' he said, pouring sparkling wine. 'Eat, drink, be merry, Angostina. Tonight is the same as our wedding night. But, as we no longer believe in God, we don't need His blessing, do we? Come along, child, why so solemn; smile. You look like you are going to your execution.'

'I feel as if I am,' she murmured. 'I don't want your rich food. How could I when the children are hungry? And, no, thank you, I don't drink alcohol.'

'Oh, cheer up. What a little goody-goody! I've come to teach you how to enjoy life's pleasures.'

'How is that possible with you?' she hissed. 'I loathe you. I despise you as a man.'

'Really?' He smiled in his precise way, his razor-sharp features like a bird of prey, watching her through his slanted eyes. 'You will have an appetite when I have finished with you. You'll be begging for more.'

Angostina took a deep breath. 'I don't think so.'

'I know so. None so proud that can't be broken.' He swilled some wine down his throat. 'Come on, try some; you will like it.'

She shook her head, her blue eyes modestly averted. 'I don't want to.'

'Come. You mustn't be frightened of me. Try to relax. It will be so much better. Such sad eyes, such pale lips, such white skin, such shining golden hair. You don't need any beauty aids,

Angostina, no kohl, no rouge, no powder. You are adorable. You have such a beatific glow to your beauty, it shines from you. But you are not untouchable. Ah, no, you are far from that.'

The captain suddenly leaned over and gripped her thigh, then ripped up her skirt to reveal her legs and underclothes. Angostina almost cried out but braced herself. His fingers were like some poisonous creature that was creeping up under her pantelettes. She clamped her hand on his to restrain him and saw that his tongue was protruding through his thin lips, pink and obscene, a dribble of wine on his chin, and he was grinning at her, devilishly. 'Oh, I am going to touch you, Angostina, touch you everywhere. I want to see you, all of you.'

'Why? Why must you be so lewd?' She tried to fight him off as he suddenly stood and attacked her. She gave a sharp scream as he tried to kiss her. '*Non me molesta!*'

'You didn't want it easy, did you?' he shouted. 'Right. You can have it the hard way.' He snatched a coil of her short hair and slapped her viciously across the face. 'We will feast afterwards. First things first.'

He dragged her screaming and fighting over to the big bed and threw her upon it. He pinned her down, breathing heavily. 'You will open to me, girl. Or I will have my soldiers come in and hold you down, then I will throw you to them.'

She lay like a statue staring at him, defiantly. 'How can you be so foul?' Then she closed her eyes and began to pray.

'It's no use praying,' he sneered. 'He won't help you.'

'Won't he?' a voice asked. 'Well, maybe I will.'

Captain Romero froze in his tracks, standing over Angostina in his uniform and boots. 'What?' He swivelled his head around to look at the big chamber, the open window, but there was no one there. He shook his head, sharply. Maybe it was the drink? Maybe he had imagined it?

He smiled cruelly and unbuttoned his holster, drawing his revolver. 'You virgin nuns, you make me sick,' he shouted, obsessed by the sight of her. 'First I am going to deflower you with this and then — '

Angostina screamed and fought as, like a man possessed, he began tearing and ripping her grey robe and under-clothes from her, kneeling over her, kissing frantically at her face, her neck, her exposed pale breasts.

'Maybe that ain't a good idea.'

Romero froze again as he heard the voice. This time it spoke not Spanish, but English. He turned slowly and saw the *gringo* hauling himself through the narrow casement window.

'Howdy,' he grinned, as he jumped through.

He was a man with black hair hanging about his harsh, dark face, dressed in a ragged leather coat, jeans and boots. Captain Romero raised his revolver, cocked it, and fired. But, he was too late. Slaughter's Schofield was out of its holster a split second before, and he ducked as he anticipated the shot, which whistled harmlessly past his head. Slaughter fanned three bullets into the *jefe politico* on the bed, making him throw up his arms in a strange moaning and jerking ejaculation of death.

For moments, Slaughter was lost in his terrible memory, the night he returned from the war, found the Yankee officer in bed with his young wife, killed him as he went for his gun, then, unable to cease, turned his gun on the screaming, begging girl, and killed her, too. This night he stood there in his nightmare staring at the dead, lolling officer, at the half-naked blonde girl by his side, staring at him, and he turned his revolver on her, too. For seconds he stared at her, his finger taking first pressure on the trigger, then he blinked, shook his head.

'Hey, what's the matter with me?'

He holstered the smoking Schofield, hauled the dead Romero crashing to the floor, then lay down beside her, putting his boots up. 'Hey, whadda ya know?'

'My God!' Angostina cried. 'Who are you? Where on earth did you come from?'

'Through the window.'

'No, I mean' — she tried to cover her nakedness — 'where before that?'

'Waal,' he drawled, rolling off the bed and taking a long swig from the bottle of wine, his Adam's apple jerking in his strong neck. 'We was riding up from Santa Julia along the lakeside when we saw this bunch of men, two or three of 'em in uniform, the rest Juaristas, red sashes round their waists. We followed 'em from a distance and saw 'em file into this here convent, whatever it is.'

'Orphanage.'

'Well, I had business here, too, so I wondered what they was up to. When it came dark I decided to investigate. I took my lariat and managed to hook it over one of the buttresses above this room. I hauled myself up and, lo and behold, what did I see — a sight for sore eyes, a blonde beauty praying to God to rescue her from a fate worse than death. So, seeing as it's generally agreed in this new republic that there ain't no God no more, I thought it was up to me to play His part and intervene.'

He grinned, lecherously, at the girl, her long, pale limbs exposed, *au naturelle*. 'Do you think He might reward me in Heaven? Or should I claim my reward now?'

He stared through narrowed eyes at the frightened girl and it was as if she could read his thoughts.

'No, please,' she pleaded. 'What do you want here?'

'I'm looking for a certain Angostina del Briganza de Apuarte.'

'What do you want with me?'

'Well now' — he took another swig from the bottle and gave her the once over — 'what could any man want with a beaut like you? You sure got our friend here in a fine lather.'

'Please,' she said, 'be serious.'

'I am serious. I brought you a present from your father, thassall. He's paid me to.'

'My father, but I haven't seen him since — '

Suddenly there was the sound of voices, of men running up the spiral staircase, alerted by the gunshots, a hammering on the door with a rifle butt. '*Capitan*, are you all right?'

'Sure, he's fine. I've sent him to a better place, I hope. Come on in.'

Slaughter ducked down behind the bed as the door burst open and two soldiers tumbled in, their rifles at the ready, staring at the girl, and around the room.

Slaughter stood up. 'Hi,' he called. He fanned the Schofield's hammer again and they danced in a dance of death, tumbling to the floor.

Angostina, lying on the bed, stared

horrified. 'What are you doing? You can't kill everybody.'

'Can't I?' He strode over to the door, reloading the revolver. 'Stay here.'

* * *

When he was gone the young woman stared aghast at the bodies of the dead men, blood flowing from them, Romero, his face drawn back in a retch of agony. She was ashamed of her relief that he was dead. She did not even wish to pray for his departed soul that must surely be condemned to wander in purgatory. She slipped off the bed, carefully avoiding the bodies. Her mouth was so dry, she needed a drink. She tipped the remains of the bottle into a glass and sipped at it. It was fizzy and pleasant, lifting her spirits. Who was this man? What did he want with her? There was the muffled roar of an explosion from outside, shouts of alarm, sounds of shooting. Quickly, she thought: I must go to protect the children.

Slaughter had still been carrying the keg of gunpowder on his pack-horse. When he and his two *compadres* saw the twenty Juaristas enter the convent they had waited until dark and crept forward on foot. There were two or three guards posted on the battlements of the outer wall, but they were smoking cigarettes, not paying much attention. Slaughter had pulled the bung from the barrel, fixed in a length of fuse, and nodded at Swanger as he put the cask outside the big, wooden, outer gateway. 'There's something funny going on up at that lighted window. I heard a scream. I'm gonna climb up and take a look. Gimme fifteen minutes then blow this gate in and come in shootin'. OK, pal?'

'Sure. We were with Gen'ral Forrest, weren't we? The greatest guerilla fighter of them all. Leave it to us.'

Slaughter had swirled his lariat to land on a buttress of the tower above the chamber and began to haul himself up, his boots scraping on the stone wall . . .

Now, he was running down the circular staircase when he heard the gate go up and at the same time two soldiers came running up towards him. When they came around the corner he fanned four shots from his Schofield and gave them a one-way ticket to perdition.

Outside, Abel had used his own lariat to scale the convent wall and slid silently over the battlements. He saw the glow of a cigarette and the dark shape in the starlight of a guard standing with his back to him. He drew his pig-sticker, crept forward, and stuck it in his throat, muffling the cry with his gloved hand. He could see another guard with a rifle on the far wall. He levered a bullet into his own carbine and took him out as the big gate was blown to smithereens.

Seth Swanger didn't have the figure for scaling walls. He ran through the main gate shielded by the cloud of dust and debris, shooting at every Juarista who stepped out before him, levering his carbine and firing with years of accustomed ease. Men threw up their hands and fell before him. When his twelve shots were gone he tossed the carbine aside and drew his revolver as soldiers ran out from the stables and the house.

Up on the battlements, Abel cut them down as they ran out into the yard. 'It's like potting ducks,' he giggled. He saw a guard with a bayonet running to stab Swanger in the back and he shot him down, too. But, by then his magazine was empty, so he leaped from the battlements onto the back of another guard who was about to bayonet Seth. Unluckily for Abel, the guard looked up and saw him coming and his bayonet, instead, went through the little hillbilly's belly and out the other side.

Slaughter had paused in the chapel to reload, but as he dashed into the convent kitchen he saw two uniformed soldiers firing from the doorway. He picked up a tureen of boiling water and hurled it at them. They howled and turned to him and he gritted his teeth, fanned the hammer again and sent them tumbling out into the yard.

By the time he stepped out onto the cobbles it was all over. Swanger was standing over the guard who had bayoneted his pal Abel, finishing him with a bullet to the brain. He looked down at the eviscerated Funt. 'For a li'l guy he had a lot of guts.'

Suddenly Angostina had run out into the courtyard. 'What are you doing?' she cried. 'Don't you give anyone a chance to surrender?'

'Well, it ain't likely they would have extended that courtesy to us,' Slaughter replied. 'What's the matter with you? Ain't you glad to be rescued?'

'Yes, but I did not want this. These men, they are just soldiers. They should not have to pay for their captain's sins.'

'Everybody has to pay, especially if

they back the wrong side. They musta known what he was up to. Now, do you think you could do us a favour — fix us some cawfee?'

She stared at him with her frank blue eyes and frowned. 'Of course.'

'Right. I'll go get the hosses,' he called to Swanger, reloading his Schofield from his belt and stepping around in his catlike way in case there might be an enemy still out there in the shadows. Then he prowled out through the debris of the shattered gateway.

'To tell you the truth,' he said to his mustang when he found him along beside the lakeside. 'I ain't sure how we're gonna explain this to the authorities.'

When he got back to the convent leading the mounts, he hauled one of the sacks of silver ingots from one of the horses. He slung it over his shoulder, pushed into the kitchen and dumped it on the table where Angostina was pouring coffee into clay mugs.

'There y'are. A present from your pa. Fifty thousand pesos in silver.'

Angostina picked up one of the slim ingots and stared at it. 'What . . . where . . . how did you get this?'

'At considerable risk to our lives. Don't you ever say thank-you for anythang?'

'I can't accept this.'

'Why not? It's silver honestly mined. You could call it your father's conscience money. Look on it as your dowry, gal.'

'If you don't want it, lady,' Swanger said, with his gappy smile, 'I'd be glad to take it off your hands.'

'I don't know what to do. I've never seen so — '

At that point Maria and the other old nun came into the kitchen with a crowd of children curious to know if the new war was over.

'Sure it is. Just a little misunderstanding,' Slaughter told them, and winked at Angostina. 'You know that silver would buy these kids an awful lot of treats. Step into the real world, gal.'

'But what can I do with it?'

'If I was you I'd find a damn good hiding place first of all. Then, now and again, take a bar into Durango. There's plenty of buyers for silver, give you cash, no questions asked. You're rich. Cain't you get that into your head?'

For the first time she smiled, warmly, at him as she ruffled the hair of the children who had come to sit round her. 'Well, children, I think we must say thank-you to the American, Señor — ?'

'Slaughter.'

'Slaughter. We won't be hungry any more. And the orphanage will go from strength to strength. Shall we sing a song for him?'

Even the hard-bitten James Slaughter had to smile and wipe a tear from his eye by the time that ordeal was done. 'I'm gonna turn in,' he said. 'It's been a hard day. I'll take that bed up in the tower chamber. I'll chuck them other galoots outa the window. You wouldn't care to jine me, would ya, Angostina?'

'I'm not that grateful,' she smiled. 'Mr Slaughter.'

10

A rumble of thunder reached their ears the next morning as they loaded the dead *jefe politico* and his *Juaristas* onto their horses and led them across to a ravine in the hills behind the convent. They tipped the fly-buzzing bodies into it and scattered their rifles about to try to make it look as if they had died in battle. The storm had been threatening all night so at least the thunder might have disguised the noise of their own battle from the ears of a nearby village a mile along the lakeside.

'If they don't git back from patrol in a week or so, somebody's gonna come looking for 'em, thass fer sure,' Swanger said, flicking the flies from his own face. 'What we hanging around fer?'

Slaughter wasn't sure of the answer to that. It would make sense to get moving as soon as they could. 'Aw, there ain't no hurry,' he growled, as he stood and looked across the lake to where the sky had darkened to gunmetal and a fine tracery of lightning streaked across the mountain crags that rose to 14,000 feet, their snow peaks protruding above the clouds.

'He was a curious li'l clodhopper,' Swanger said as he swung the last of the corpses, Abel Funt, from a bronc and stared at his ill-nourished face. 'But he knew how to fight, fornicate and git drunk. He had his fun.'

'Yeah.' Slaughter grimaced as he watched Abel go tumbling down to join the soldiers. It was a distasteful task. It did not please him to see twenty more men dead by their guns. But what choice had they had? A Mexican rarely surrendered. He would fight until all his bullets had gone and then come at you with a machete. 'Let's git outa here. I need a drink.'

'What shall we do with their broncs? Shoot 'em?'

'No. Set 'em free. Let 'em find their own way back.'

They did so, cracking their lariats and shouting at them, 'Haugh! Haugh Haugh!' The saddled mustangs moved off but, puzzled by being free and riderless, stopped and stared after the two Americans as they rode away.

The morning, in the clear air of the mountains, was magnificent on their side of the big lake, but on the far side they could see stormclouds rolling down from the passes blowing back-trails of dark downpours.

'Here comes the rains,' Swanger sang out.

'Yup. Let's get to that village before *they* do.'

They raced their horses away along the sandy edge of the placid blue waters until they reached a small collection of adobe huts. There was a rickety table and chairs on a covered terrace of a tumbledown *cantina*. Swanger and Slaughter sprawled at ease and called for *aguardiente*, literally fire-water. It looked like the bar-owner made his own, crushing sugar cane in an adjacent mangle and fermented the juice.

'*Hola, señors!*' he cried. 'You want to eat?'

'Just keep the booze comin',' Swanger beamed, taking a swig of the murky liquid and sighing. 'I need this. It's like oxygen to me.'

'Yeah.' Slaughter took a more careful gulp of the alcohol. 'It'll more likely blow your head off.'

'We got duck shot yesterday. Or fish caught this morning, tortillas, or omelettes.' The barman kissed his fingers to his lips. '*Magnifico.*'

'Gimme the duck.' Slaughter slapped a silver peso down, and spoke in Spanish, 'You got any questions to ask me before you go?'

'No, *señor*, what questions would I have? Life is quiet here.'

'Good, I'm glad to hear that.'

He was watching fishermen pulling up their canoes and cleaning their nets when the rains hit, running across the waters and turning them grey; fierce rods churning it; running across the sand and rattling down on the canopy of maize leaves above their heads. Men, women and children scurried to take cover around them. They were clear-eyed, healthy folk, no doubt due to their diet of fish and wildfowl.

Slaughter was scooping up the chilli juices about the remains of his roast duck with a thin tortilla when he saw Angostina walking along the lakeside, leading a crocodile of shaven-headed orphans in their blue smocks. It was early afternoon and the rain had eased.

'Hey, here she comes,' Swanger chuckled. 'You seen the breasts on her? Whoo! I could sure teach that gal a thang or two.'

'Ain't you got no respect?' Slaughter growled. 'She used to be a nun. She's the daughter of an aristocrat. She ain't fer the likes of you.'

'Yeah, you dirty bastard. I bet you're plannin' to git yer own hands on her. Thass what you're hangin' round fer. I know you. You allus was a crafty one.'

'You misjudge me,' Slaughter replied, and began braying with laughter. 'That's a real cruel thang to say.'

Angostina saw them and waved, but her procession weaved on past them to the village stores. He saw her bartering for fish and fruit and loading it into baskets. He had changed one of her silver bars for a pile of pesos. She was not to know he had found them in the pockets of Romero and his soldiers. When she began her return journey he beckoned to her to join them. 'Ain't you got business to attend to, Swanger?' he growled.

'Yeah, I mighta known. I'll go see if I cain't find myself some fat squaw. Here's betting you don't git to first base with this lady.'

He touched his hat to Angostina when she arrived, and ambled away. 'See ya later.'

Angostina had left the children to play on the sand. She sat beside him on the spare chair. Today she was dressed in a lemon-coloured peasant blouse which revealed her slim arms and the enticing shadowed valley between her formidable bosom. Her bare legs protruded from a dark bell-shaped skirt.

'That don't look like no nun's outfit.'

'I'm not a nun any longer. I never really wanted to be one. But when my mother died there was nowhere else to go.'

'You could have gone back to your father.'

'I was told he was a bad man,' she said, casting her eyes down. 'I did not think he would want me.'

'Do you want to come with me to visit him?'

'How can I leave the children? He is welcome to visit me here. Thank him for his gift. It will be put to good use.'

'Watcha having?' Slaughter asked, raising a stone mug of *aquardiente*.

'I don't drink alcohol. It is the curse of Mexico. But I must admit I had a drop of the wine you left last night. It was nice.' Her blue eyes widened as she stared at him. 'It made me feel strange.'

'Yeah,' he smiled, 'I guess it would. How about the divine berry of Jalapa, as they call it. You aginst that, too?'

'Coffee? No, I love it. I had never tasted it until I gave up my vows.'

'I guess there's a lot of thangs you ain't never tasted?' Slaughter called out to the bar-owner to bring the lady a best Jalapa-state coffee. 'I could suggest a few more.'

Her pale hair had been cropped close when she was a nun, but since then she had enjoyed letting it grow more luxuriantly. 'To tell you the truth I feel wonderfully free of restrictions since throwing off my nun's clothes. Today, for the first time, I put on this more feminine blouse and skirt. It makes me feel gay. I know, after those shocking events last night, all those men you killed, I should *not* feel like this, but I do. The children can eat again. And the coming of the rains after all the dust and drought always makes us feel happy.'

'Aw, and there was me thinkin' you mighta got your glad rags on on my account. They suit you, that's for sure.'

'Thank you, but you flatter yourself, Mr Slaughter.' Angostina could not, however, prevent a blush creeping into her pale cheeks. 'I hope you don't think . . . no, you're teasing me.'

'Well, I'm happy you're happy. I thought maybe you might be upset. We tried to clean up the mess.'

'Yes, so I saw. I know I should not say this, but that man, Romero, I'm glad he is dead. I hated that man. He was loathsome, utterly corrupt.'

'Them ain't very nun-like feelings.'

'I can't help it. That's how I feel.' She sipped at her coffee as the children crowded round and she found them a handful of *centavos* to go buy candied cakes. 'You must think me odd.'

'Well, yeah,' Slaughter drawled, pouring a coffee for himself. 'I wasn't expecting to find such an honest and outspoken young lady. Tell me,' he said, lighting a cheroot, 'do you really believe all that religious hogwash?'

'Hogwash? I could hardly describe it as that. But' — she gave her wide, fresh-faced smile — 'I have had my doubts.'

'About what?'

'Parthenogenesis, for one instance.'

'Partheno-what?'

'Virgin birth. I mean, is it possible? And why is the virgin so idolized? To imbue us with a sense of guilt about the sexual act?'

'Could be.' Slaughter gave a whistle of awe. 'You young wimmin certainly call a spade a spade these days. And you? You're one, I presume.'

'A virgin, yes. But I haven't given birth.'

Slaughter gave a hoot of laughter. 'You could make a fortune in a sideshow if you did.'

'I'm not joking, Mr Slaughter. I am not a fool. My mother schooled me before I went to the nuns. I am a believer, but I find it difficult to accept all the pomp and riches of the church when in reality there is so much poverty. Nor can I see why we should be ruled by some old priest thousands of miles away across the sea? Why should his decrees be thought infallible?'

'Well, I *ain't* a believer, and I've had my doubts on those lines, too. But, I thought you people took the whole package without question. Maybe you oughta start your own church. Up north of the border we do it all the time. Why, up in Salt Lake City there's an old fella got hisself sixty wives and he says its according to the divine word of the Lord. All his disciples are digging away making the desert flourish and the gov'ment cain't do nuthin' about it. Maybe you should forget about the Roman Catholic Church, call yourself the Mexican Catholic Church. Mexico for the Mexicans, ain't that what everybody's saying?'

'You may have a point, Mr Slaughter. *Viva independencia*, isn't that the slogan?'

'I wish you'd call me James.'

Angostina reminded him of a freshly sliced grapefruit, so sparkling and clean and clear-eyed and, yes, sharply succulent. She sat straight-backed, eager to discuss matters she could never have spoken about to anyone before, certainly not a man.

'I'm afraid that would be too familiar,' she said. 'I'm sorry, I didn't mean to . . . perhaps I ought to go. The children — '

'Aw, forget the children. It's great to talk to you.'

It was very pleasant, lazing there, looking out over the lake, which was a sparkling blue again, to the mountains beyond. A kitten was playing in the canopy above their heads splashing drops of rainwater down on them. It was one of those times a man would remember all his life. He did not wish to break the spell, but he felt impelled to.

'So, as we're being so frank, I've sometimes wondered, do nuns ever think about sex, about men? Did you?'

'Of course,' she shrugged, with a smile. 'I have been guilty of lustful thoughts.'

'About who?'

She stared out over the lake, silent for a while. 'It is so sad,' she murmured, 'to see the little church in this village locked up, people forbidden to enter. The *peons*, the Indians, they need religion for their fiestas, their baptisms, their weddings. I sometimes think it is like a drug to them.'

'You're changing the subject.'

'All right, yes, I had lustful thoughts about a priest.'

'A priest?'

'Yes, but he was — he is — young, well-built, very handsome, with a shock of curly hair. A very idealistic man. I first met him when he came to the convent and, I have to admit, I melted with fear and desire.'

'So, did he feel the same?'

'I don't know' — she shook her head, sharply — 'perhaps, no, of course he didn't. How could he? He is very devout.'

'He's a man, ain't he? They say a quarter of the kids in Mexico are fathered by priests.'

'No. He's not like that. Although once, I was so enamoured, I was thinking of going to offer myself. I listened outside his chamber door. He was praying, crying out, and it sounded as if he was whipping himself.'

'Tryin' to thrash out the old Adam. Of course, he fancied you, gal.'

'No, I don't think he could have been like that.'

'Who is he? Where is he now?'

'He is a priest on the run, in hiding. His father superior, Father Francisco, was shot by the revolutionaries in Santa Julia. Now Juan — Juan Caldo is his name — goes about giving absolution, hearing confessions, baptizing children into the family of the church. Oddly enough, last night Arsenio Romero told me they had heard he was in this district, they were confident they would catch him, put him before a firing squad. I pray that he has got away, gone to join the *Christeros* up in the mountains. They are a religious movement fighting against the revolution.'

'A gang of fanatics, I heard.' Slaughter stroked his grey chin. 'But I also heard that if priests give up their vows they will be allowed to live in peace. If they throw away their cassocks they'll be appointed teachers in schools, as long as they vow not to preach religion. You could marry him.'

'Juan would not agree to that. It would be too humiliating.'

'He'd rather be harried from pillar to post? More fool him when he's got a beautiful and intelligent girl like you crazy about him.'

'I did not say I was crazy about him,' she smiled. 'I just said I once had very lustful thoughts about him. I have tried to overcome them.'

'Yeah, well, you do that. But it seems like a hell of a waste of a good woman to me.'

'I must be going, James.' She was rising, politely shaking his hand. 'It has been very interesting talking to you. I feel as if I have been to confession. I must be getting the children back for their supper. I know you are a man who kills for money, but I believe, underneath, you are a good man.'

'Gee, thanks,' he drawled, holding on to her fingers for as long as he could until he let her slip away from him. 'But I wouldn't put too much money on that if I were you.'

He watched her gathering up the orphans and setting off along the shore. 'Hell take her,' he said. 'What am I gettin' involved with her for?' He called to the barman, 'Let's have some more of that *aquardiente*.'

11

A crowd of Indians had converged on the village the next day. They were decorated with feathers, banging drums and cymbals, intent on holding a *fiesta* for some saint or other. They broke into the church and poured inside, chanting and wailing.

'What would Mexico be without religion and gunpowder?' Slaughter mused as he listened to the racket as Indian children starting throwing fireworks.

'Yeah, or *aquardiente*,' Swanger grinned.

Swanger, Slaughter and Angostina sat outside the *cantina* and watched the Indians troop from the church bearing aloft their painted idols. They were swaying and chanting, as if possessed, drunk or drugged, arranged the wooden statuettes in a circle and began dancing.

'Let's all git drunk,' Swanger beamed,

and streamed *aquardiente* down his throat from a goatskin.

'You were born drunk,' Slaughter said. 'But, hey, how about joining in the dance?'

He stood, raising his muscular arms, clicking his fingers, taking a stance, and smiled at Angostina. 'Come on, give it a whirl.'

'I don't know how to,' she protested.

'Aw, just do what comes natural.' He pulled her to her feet, tossing his hat down. 'You dance around it. Just do what the others do. Go with the music.'

She, too, raised her arms, swayed her body, stepping back and forth, her skirt swirling as she spun around the hat. She had never been allowed to smile before. She had often been chided for chattering and smiling in the convent and made to kneel for hours before the altar as punishment. But now she felt as if she were floating, her whole body finding its true expression, celebrating the joy of life, and her smile widened, her cheeks flushed, as she met Slaughter's eyes.

'Yeah, you've got the rhythm,' he called, and stepped forward, took her in his arms and whirled her in more of a Texas two-step than the intricate Indian dance.

Gradually he whirled her out of the throng and into the shade of an alleyway between two *casas*. He pressed her up against an adobe wall, knew her breasts warm and resilient against his chest, put a strong hand at the back of her head and kissed her hard and long as if he were feeding on some delicious fruit.

Angostina at first was too surprised to resist, and curious, too, but when she felt his tongue probing into her lips, his hand pulling her dress up her thighs, she shook her head trying to break from his embrace.

'No, please.' Turning her face away she gasped for air. He had persuaded her to attend the *fiesta*, leave the children at the orphanage, and now she knew why. 'You are like an animal.

What do you think you can do — have me here?'

'Aw, come on, relax. It's only a li'l kiss.' He held her tight, running his hands up her waist and abdomen, pressing her breasts up high, trying to get his mouth to them.

'No!' she cried, struggling with the powerfully built American. 'Please, it is no good. I cannot do this. You and I we come from different worlds.'

He stared at her through his slits of eyes, breathing hard, tempted to take her against her will. 'Jeez,' he hissed. 'Don't you know what you do to a man?'

Angostina's ice-blue eyes met his deep-set green ones with a strange defiance. She was breathing hard, too. 'I should not have come here.' She straightened her blouse and skirt as he stepped back. 'I must go back to the orphanage.'

'Yeah, I guess you should,' he growled, 'if that's where you belong. Go on, then, go, 'fore I change my mind.'

Angostina brushed her hair from her eyes, gave him an apologetic smile, and slipped away. Slaughter rested his back against the wall in the shade for a while. Then he went out and picked up his hat, stepping through the drunken Indians who would go on dancing all night.

He wandered down to the lake shore and looking along saw her slim figure, a *mantilla* around her hair, hurrying back towards the stone convent on its outcrop of rock. He took off his boots and gunbelt and dived headlong into the icy water, kicking, flailing, attempting to douse the fires that coursed through his veins.

When he staggered out, he climbed up to the terrace of the *cantina*, squeezed out his shirt, put it over a chair back to dry, and called for a drink. Eventually, when he had calmed, he went to find Swanger, hauled him out of the throng and said, 'Come on. We're getting out of here.'

★ ★ ★

A shocking sight greeted them when they rode their mustangs through the shattered gate into the courtyard of the convent. Angostina was standing on tiptoe on a chair with a noose tight around her throat, the rope-end tossed around the spur of a buttress and tied to the saddle-horn of a paunchy rider in a big sombrero, bandoliers of bullets around his shoulders, a rifle clutched in one hand, pointed at the girl.

'What in tarnation — ' Swanger gasped.

'*Aiyee, greengos!*' A voice called. 'Remember me?'

Slaughter looked around and saw the skinny *bandido* chief, in a peaked officer's cap, his mouthful of ill-fitting gold teeth grinning at him. He was standing in the shadow of the kitchen doorway, a carbine in one hand, the other holding up a sack of silver.

'We heard you here,' the *captain* chuckled. 'We like vairy much what we find. We been waiting for you.'

Angostina's jaw was jerked to one

side, and she teetered, taking the pressure as the man on horseback jerked viciously on the rope.

Slaughter's eyes glimmered in their slits as he sat straight-backed on his mustang and looked around him. From what he could note there were a dozen of them, lounging indolently at various points around the courtyard, grinning insolently, their guns at the ready.

'Let her go,' he said. 'This ain't nuthin' to do with her.'

'Aha, *greengo*. First we gonna let her watch us keel you. Then, maybe, we all take turn with her. But' — he dropped the silver and pointed a finger — 'you make one bad move we *hang* her.'

Seeing the stymied look on the faces of the two Americans as they sat their horses and raised their hands, the bandit chief strutted over to Angostina, reached up and ripped her blouse away. Her hands tied behind her back, she had to stand on the chair, palely naked, as he tore her skirt away, too, and his men laughed and cheered, lecherously.

'She is beauty-fool, eh, *greengo*? We are gon' to have fun with her. Just theenk what you mees, huh!' The *jefe* waggled his tongue between his gold teeth and glowered. 'You theenk you can keel my *amigos* and get away from me? Nobody does that to El Lobo and live.'

Angostina opened her parched lips to plead, 'Please you won't hurt the children, will you?'

'No, we no hurt children. Wha' you theenk we are, peegs?' He grinned at the Americans. 'Now, you two, step down from your horses. We gonna have fun with you before we keel you. First you unbuckle your gunbelts . . . vairy slowly . . . toss them away . . . Mind, no treeks. Or she goes. You ready, Manuel?'

He reached up, giggling, and stroked one of the girl's legs. 'You don't want her to die, do you?'

'OK, *jefe*, you win.' Slaughter watched Manuel tighten his hold on the noose rope. 'You can have our guns. No tricks. OK by you, pal?' He glanced at Swanger on his left. 'You know what to do?'

'Sure,' Swanger grinned. 'Looks like these filthy greasers got us bush-whacked, don't it?'

Slaughter slowly moved his hand across to his belt buckle as if about to obey and brought the Schofield out fast as greased lightning, fanning the hammer and toppling one . . . two . . . three of the Mexicans before they could get out a shot.

Simultaneously, Swanger concentrated on the lefthand side, spinning his horse around and his Colt .45 sent three *bandidos* spinning into eternity.

El Lobo gave a high-pitched yelp of rage and fear and kicked the chair away from Angostina to leave her kicking on the end of the rope, bringing up his carbine and firing at Slaughter as his mustang bore down on him, but he was bowled over.

Slaughter caught the girl in one arm and held her up as he sent a slug ploughing into Manuel's chest, cart-wheeling him from his horse.

By now the remaining Mexicans were letting loose a fusillage at the two horsemen. Swanger's horse whinnied with fear, rising on its back-legs, kicking out. One of its forehooves caught *El Lobo*, splitting his head into a bloody mess. A bullet slammed into Swanger's chest, dislodging him from the saddle. He hit the ground hard, and lay there, watching, as Slaughter held his big revolver arm's-length and took out two of the wildly firing bandits without hesitation.

Slaughter hung onto Angostina's warm, naked body, pressing her to his chest, and kneed his mustang swirling around.

'Look out!' Swanger gasped, seeing a swarthy-faced man rising from behind a water trough, his rifle aimed at Slaughter's back. Slaughter swung round to face him but — he realized — his six shots were spent.

With immense effort, Swanger raised his Colt Frontier and fired his last bullet. Unerringly it burrowed between the Mexican rifleman's eyes whose shot went wild as he screamed in agony and toppled into the trough.

Slaughter looked around him, apprehensively, but all dozen bandits were sprawled in attitudes of death as the black gunsmoke drifted. He hung on to the girl, jerked his Bowie from his belt and cut the rope above her head as Manuel's mustang tugged away, keeping it tight. He gently lowered her to the ground.

'Whoo!' He whistled out his breath, looked down at the gold-toothed *jefe* and hurled the knife to stick into his chest. 'They ought have called him El Loco not El Lobo.'

He glanced across at Swanger. 'You OK, pal?'

But the big man was clutching at his shirt, soggy with blood from the hole in his chest. 'Yeah,' he coughed out. 'That larned 'em not to tangle with Forrest's boys.'

Slaughter jumped down on one knee beside him. 'Hail, that don't look good.'

'Aw, thass OK. It's the way I allus wanted to go, with a gun in my hand and my boots on. I wouldn't have it any other way.'

'You're a brave man, Swanger. One of the best.' Slaughter lit a cheroot, let the smoke trickle out of his lips and passed it to the dying man. There was no way he could help him. 'Is there anyone I should tell?'

'Nope. I ain't got nobody. Ain't it a shame? Just when we git our hands on a grubstake, all that silver.'

'Yeah.' Slaughter offered his hand and gripped his. 'Still, you saved this lady's life, that's what you did. Without you she'd be dead. The gen'ral would be proud of you.'

'Yeah?' Swanger tried to swivel his eyes up towards Angostina, to say something, but he slumped back, life passing from him. He died with a smile on his face.

Maria had come from the kitchen, wrapped a poncho around the half-naked girl and escorted her indoors.

She sat shivering, staring at her hands. 'He is a strange man,' she murmured. 'On the one hand a callous, hired killer. But on the other, he is kind and tender.'

★ ★ ★

It was dark by the time James Slaughter had loaded up all the bandits and ditched them in the ravine. The vultures had already made a nice mess of the soldiers but it would look more like a real fight now. He wondered, in an abstract, professional way, if there was any money on the head of El Lobo, but then grinned to himself. What did he need more cash for? He'd got enough to buy and stock a nice little spread. A big silver moon was climbing high and the stars sparkling, the air fresh from that morning's rain. It was time to hit the trail.

When he got back to the convent the old ex-nun, Maria, had put the children to bed and fried him up a meal of fish and *frijoles*. 'How's Angostina?'

'She is resting.'

Maria said she, too, was going to bed, so he bade her goodnight. 'I'll be leaving in the morning.'

He sat alone in the kitchen for a while, drinking coffee, thinking about what had occurred, what might occur when he got to Don Arturo's. 'There's something about that guy that don't add up,' he muttered. 'He said he hadn't signed away his lands, but that other galoot said he had.'

He got to his feet, threw his gunbelt over his shoulder, took a candle and climbed up the spiral staircase to the big bed-chamber. He might as well, he thought, sleep in comfort. When he pushed through the door he saw Angostina, in a white nightdress, lying on the bed. 'Waal,' he drawled, 'this is a surprise. Am I in the wrong room?'

'No.' She held out a hand to him, her vivid blue eyes fearful but challenging. 'I want to thank you.'

'You don't need to.' He put the candle aside, sat down on the edge of the bed beside her. 'It might not be a good idea.'

'I want you,' she hissed, putting her arms out to him. 'I wanted you from the first moment I saw you — when you climbed through that window.'

'Yeah?' His dark face split into deep grooves as he grinned. 'That's funny, so did I.' He twisted himself agilely around and on top of her. 'I mean I wanted you.'

* * *

They made love again in the morning and it was easier and more relaxed than their violent struggles of the night. 'James,' she said, clutching him to her. 'That man, Swanger, he told me that you killed your wife, that's why you can never settle down. Is that true?'

'Yep.' He tugged at the ends of his thin moustache, sucking at his teeth. 'I guess it is.'

'You live in turmoil. Tell me, how did it happen?'

'Like most things — stupid, tragic things — on the spur of the moment, in thoughtless fury. Why does anyone kill? As if possessed, by instinct?'

'Kill the one they love?'

'Loved.' He sighed and rolled onto his back, staring at the ceiling. 'She was young, only fifteen, and me, not much older, sixteen, when war broke out. I was Texan by birth, but my family had moved on to New Mexico to homestead a fertile piece of land. I was wild and hot to join Wharton's Texan brigade. Angelina begged me to marry her and swore to wait for me while I was away. I guess it was the thought of her waiting for me kept me going through all the horror.'

He paused, for he had never spoken about this to anyone before. 'Yes, go on,' she urged.

'I wrote to her when I could but it was difficult. We were in the midst of non-stop campaigns, penetrating deep behind the enemy lines, Kentucky, Tennessee, Mississippi. I had never killed a man before, but soon shooting down some unlucky soldier was no more to me than slaughtering a hog. The retreat to Selma was the bloodiest fighting of all.'

'That's when the South surrendered?'

'Yeah. On our western side. They had thrown in the towel over in the east. We were down to old men and boys. We couldn't go on. Anyhow, when I got mustered out I crossed the Mississippi, bought a ten-dollar horse and made my way back through Comanche country to New Mexico. It took a while. Maybe she thought I wasn't coming back. It must have been hard on her.'

'What happened?'

'It was all quiet when I rode into my father's farm. I went into the house and there she was, in bed, in the arms of some Yankee officer. I shot him as he went for his revolver hung on the bed-head. I could not stop. She was screaming and pleading with me. I saw the pain and fear in her honey-brown eyes and I put the second bullet between them. She lay back, dead, blood trickling down her face.'

He reached up for his own revolver in the gunbelt hung on the bedpost, put it to his ear and listened as he clicked the cylinder around. 'This is the gun I used. My Schofield. Every time I kill a man I think of her.'

She was silent for a while looking at his handsome, if harsh, rutted face, the pride and sadness of the Comanche in it. 'So, what did you do?' she whispered.

'I gave myself up. They gave me a civilian trial. The prosecutor wanted to hang me. But no Southern jury was going to hang a returning hero for killing a hated bluebelly officer.' He gave a shrug of his arms and a caustic laugh. 'They fined me two thousand dollars. That's when I became a bounty hunter. There were plenty of frontier scum to bring in — rustlers, robbers, rapists, murderers. Only, generally, I didn't bring 'em in. I hunted 'em down and killed them, without feeling, like an automaton. And every time I killed one it was like I was killing her again.'

'You poor man.' Angostina lay her head on his bare, bronze chest and kissed him, tenderly. 'What have you done to yourself?'

'You know them carousels they have on travelling fair-grounds? Well, it's like I got on one and it would never stop, I could never get off. The carousel of death.'

'Don't be stupid. Of course you can stop.'

'Yeah, well, this was going to be my last job. I felt sorry for your father, but I ain't so sure this is a good idea. People are going down like skittles. Both my pals gone and by the law of averages my turn's overdue.'

Angostina raised herself on her elbows and stared at him, her pale breasts resting on his wide chest. 'That's what this *is* for you, isn't it? A suicide trip. You can't forgive yourself.'

He shrugged again, his dark eyes staring into hers of blue, as the sunbeams through the open casement sparkled in her short-cropped hair like a halo of gold. 'Perhaps.'

'What is the matter with you? You were provoked. You acted foolishly, without thinking. You said so yourself. You have paid your price. You have your whole life in front of you. Isn't it time to start to live?'

'You're right.' He rolled her over onto her back and gripped her tight. 'That's just what I intend to do. You're damnably beautiful.'

He took her savagely, but tenderly, too, and, when he was done, he lay upon her, her perspiring palms in his. He could feel her heart pounding against his. 'You know what you said about confession,' he murmured, 'well, it's like that for me, too. It's like a huge bag of guilt I've been carrying around on my shoulders has suddenly burst. I feel free again.'

Angostina smiled at him. 'That's good.'

'To tell you the truth I had already

decided to change my life. I'm going to buy a piece of land and settle down.' He studied her, quizzically. 'Would you come with me, north of the border, marry me?'

The girl shook her head, blinking away her tears. 'I'm sorry. I can't do that.'

'Don't tell me.' He rolled away and reached for his shirt. 'You can't leave these kids.'

'How could I?'

'Waal,' he said, as he watched her get dressed. 'I jest ain't cut out to be the superintendent of an orphanage. Is that what you're goin' to do with your life?'

She turned to him, met his eyes. 'I just want to do some good for the less fortunate, look after children, be a teacher, or nurse. Is that so wrong?'

'No, course not. But, you know, one of these days the church will regain its power, the old regime will get in. Juarez can't live for ever. You thought of that? You'll never be able to be a nun again — not after this.'

'I know. I don't want to be. I just want to be myself.'

'Waal, I guess it's time I was moving on. I gotta go see your father, see what's going on.'

'James,' she said, reaching to squeeze his hand. 'Be careful. Seth told me something else. He said there are two men looking for you, friends of that officer. They have vowed to kill you.'

'Sure, I know. That's one reason I came to Mexico to fight for Juarez. But I'm through with running. If they find me, so be it, it's in the hands of the fates.'

He buckled on the Schofield, picked up his Winchester, and pulled up the collar of his leather coat. 'Listen to that damn rain pounding down again. I'm gonna git wet.'

She followed him, barefoot, down to the courtyard, kissed him for the last time, watched him swing onto his horse. '*Vaya con Dios*,' she called, the rain — or were they tears? — streaming down her face.

'You better inform the authorities them bandits had a run in with them soldiers and had a shoot-out up in the ravine.'

'You look like a bandit, yourself,' she smiled.

'No, I ain't a bandit.' He rode his mustang prancing around in a circle. 'I'm a bounty hunter. I abide by the law. Or I bend it a bit. So long, gal.'

He let the mustang have his head and went jogging off, leaping over the debris of the gate, heading away along the shore of the lake towards the north. He had an appointment at the *Rancho del Oro*.

* * *

Slaughter spent the night in a shepherd's hut and dined on mutton stew. He gave a cheroot to the gnarled old man and squatted staring into the flames of his small fire. Angostina was still within him, part of him, but he knew he had to wrench himself away. It was true, what she said, they lived in different worlds. In the morning he tossed the shepherd a silver peso — it was a month's wages to him — and rode on his way.

The constant downpour made it hard going, he had to keep stopping and scraping the balls of mud from the hooves of the mustang and the pack-horse to prevent them slipping on the treacherous terrain. But, in the afternoon the rain ceased, the sun emerged from the mist and all was calm and peaceful again. It was then that he saw a young man riding towards him on a *burro*. He was well built, wearing a muddy black suit that steamed in the heat, a torn and dirty, once-white shirt, and his bare feet were bruised and bloodstained. He looked alarmed by the sight of the bounty hunter, but came on towards him. Over one arm was crooked a battered umbrella, that sign of priestly authority.

'Hold it, mister,' Slaughter drawled,

pulling out his revolver. 'Where you off to?'

'*Señor*, I go to visit my sick mother in Santa Julia. I have nothing of value. Please let me pass.'

He had a thick mop of matted curls that trickled into the beginnings of a similarly curly beard, and there was a handsome, bronzed robustness about his face, his blue eyes both fierce and gentle. He kicked his *burro* forward with his heels.

'Not so fast, buddy.' Slaughter caught hold of the rope bridle and jumped from his own horse. 'I got my doubts about you. What you got here in your bundle?'

'Nothing of any interest, *señor*.'

'Yeah?' Slaughter pulled his blanket roll apart and let the contents tumble to the ground — a silver communion cup, a purple maniple and cloth, candles, a half-full bottle of wine. 'Waal, the authorities might well be int'rested. Whaddya ya know? I caught me a real live priest.'

The young man raised his umbrella as if to strike him but Slaughter shook his head, pointing the Schofield between his eyes. 'I wouldn't do that. There's a price on your head alive or dead and I ain't fussy which way I take you in.'

The young priest sighed, hopelessly. 'Who are you?'

'James Slaughter, bounty hunter. You jest git off that moke. You, I guess, are Father Juan Caldo.'

'How did you guess?'

'Oh, they been after you a long time. You've given 'em a good run for their money. Ain't you tired of being forever hunted, on the run? You look like you been dragged through a hedge backwards. Where you been?'

Caldo slid painfully from the ass and grimaced. 'Oh, everywhere, hiding here, hiding there, living rough like a wild animal. It's been awful. But it is — it was — my duty to keep the flame alive, to perform baptisms, hear confessions, give last rites, conduct masses. The

218

people need me.'

'Hell, they don't need you. There's more important work you can do. Say, as it's gone two and I come a long way I guess we might as well bile up a cup of cawfee 'fore I take you in. Can you take a look over in them rocks, see if there's any dry kindling? I'll see if I can find my cawfee pot.'

He passed his tin cup of black steaming, tarry liquid to Caldo and tossed him a chunk of mutton the shepherd had given him and a *tortilla*. 'These *tortillas* are a tad leathery but I guess I better keep you alive so they can shoot ya.'

Slaughter grinned, amiably. 'You know, I met a damn beaut of a gal t'other day back at some convent beside a lake. No, it ain't a convent no more. She's looking after all these poor war orphans. Angostina they call her. Hey, I can tell ya, I had fun with that gal. What a body on her!'

Juan Caldo's knuckles whitened and he found it difficult to speak, his throat had gone so dry. 'You had *fun* with her?'

'Yaah, waal, she wasn't really willing, I had to kinda force her.'

'You raped her?'

'Yeah, you could call it that, why not? Mind you, I reckon once I got started she really loved it. Whoo! She's gonna make some man a fine wife.'

'You' — Caldo could hardly restrain himself from throwing a punch at Slaughter but the eye of the Schofield was again trained on him — 'you disgust me.'

'Hech! You fancy her, yourself, you know you do. You upset about me doing the nasty things to her you'd like to do?'

'You're sick. A nun. Angostina. Such a pure young girl.'

'She ain't a nun. She's given up her vows. And, if you got any sense you'll give up yourn. You seem like a nice young fella. You think I want to take you in for them to shoot you? You got one way out: if you agree to give up the priesthood, throw away your cassock, become a teacher, say, at an orphanage, they'll let you go free. Wouldn't you rather do that than be dead?'

'How could I do that? Without God I might just as well be dead. He is my life.'

'Listen, pal, don't talk such non-sense.' Slaughter glared at him as he chewed the tough mutton. '*Life* is all there is that's worth living for. That gal, Angostina, she told me, she screamed it at me — it's you she loves. And you love her, you know you do.'

'What?' Caldo stared at the American as if he were mad. 'What are you talking about?'

'Come on, you're sick of this life. Just look at you. Your mama probably told you to find a nice cushy parish and work hard and one day you'd be a bishop in a fine palace. But it ain't worked out that way. So you gotta cut your losses and start again.'

'What?'

'Whadda ya mean, what? Are you dumb, or somethang? The gal's crazy abou'cha. Go to her. Get married, have a brood of kids. Run the damn orphanage with her.'

'You *are* mad. They told me all *Americanos* were.'

'Listen.' Slaughter jumped up, picked up the religious artefacts, hurled them one by one into the rocks. 'You're finished with these. No, it ain't no use protesting. You're making me mad. Look, you'll either make me a solemn oath you'll go and do the decent thang by that gal, marry her, or — '

'Or?'

'Or' — Slaughter squinted at him through his narrowed eyes, raising the Schofield — 'I'll execute you here and now. I ain't joking.'

'No, I don't think you are.' Juan Caldo scratched at his beard. 'May I think about this for a few minutes?'

'Sure, I'll give you three.' Slaughter smiled to himself as he watched the priest pondering. 'Right, time's up.'

'I'll do what you say.' Caldo turned his fierce blue eyes on the gunman. 'But not because you threaten me. It's because I want to. It's true, I am sick of this life. I'm sick of being guilty of my natural desire. It's true, I did — I do want Angostina. I will go to her. I hope she will have me.'

'Waal, she's a tough cookie. You'll have to convince her you mean what you say, you're starting a new life together.'

'Yes, I will. You're a strange man. Did you really do what you said you did? You didn't hurt her?'

''Course I did.' Slaughter tossed the pits of the coffee onto the fire. 'And no, 'course I didn't. But you better not tell her I said that. Let her tell you herself in her own way.'

'Thank you,' Juan Caldo said, as he watched the gunfighter spring lithely into his saddle and tug his mustang away. 'What am I thanking you for?'

'Ask yourselves that in ten years' time and raise a glass to me. So long, Señor Caldo. Be good to her. Best of luck to you.'

The young priest watched him ride away, straight-backed, pushing his mustang at a steady lope, the pack horse following, up away through the rocks. 'Good Lord,' he cried, jumping on his *burro* and heading south towards the convent. 'I ought to be angry. But I feel wonderful.' In truth, he felt elated and could not wait to give himself up.

12

The oak gates of the *Rancho del Oro* were wide open as if inviting him in. Slaughter slid from his horse on the hilltop vantage point where he had paused once before and peered at it through his telescope. There were no riflemen in any of the turrets. What was going on? He frowned as he looked at his Winchester. It was a fine piece, brought out in '66, an improved version of Ben Henry's classic rifle with a spring-activated tubular magazine under the barrel. A simple, quick movement of the trigger guard lever extracted the spent cartridge and carried a fresh shell into the chamber, cocking the hammer ready for firing. In the right hands a potent weapon. It used a rimfire brass cartridge with a .44 calibre bullet powered by 28 grains of black powder. But without the correct bullet it was, of course, useless. And James Slaughter had run out of .44s.

'It looks like it's down to you an' me, old pal,' he muttered as he checked the .45s in his Schofield and adjusted the feel of it in the holster. 'Let's hope she ain't gonna start shootin' 'til we git in range.'

He slapped the mustang's powerful neck and vaulted into the saddle, finding the stirrups as he set off down the rocky trail and then went at a steady pounding lope across the barren plain towards the *hacienda*.

He slowed as he rode through the gates into the courtyard. Admittedly, it was siesta-time, but the place appeared to be deserted. A whinny from the adjacent stables told him that this was probably not so. Several horses were shuffling around in there.

'*Hola!*' he shouted. 'Anybody here?'

Eventually, Don Arturo appeared in the doorway, more elegantly dressed than he had been before, in a pearl-decorated suit of tight black velveteen, a scarlet sash and scarlet loose bow at the neck of his starched white shirt. His silver hair had been combed back, but he looked pale and frail as he greeted the bounty hunter. 'So, you have returned. What news have you?'

Slaughter had a distinct impression someone in the shadow of the doorway was holding a gun into the old man's back. 'I've done what you asked me to do. If somebody overhears this conversation it's too bad. I'm kinda tired of all the trouble it's cost me and of bein' messed about.'

'Yes.' The *haciendado* nodded his prow of nose, though he might have been prompted. 'Go on.'

'We found the mine, the treasure. A woman of your acquaintance tried to rob us but she didn't succeed. I gave six thousand pesos to Rodrigo Cruz for his pains. We found your daughter.'

'How is she?' The old man's dull eyes brightened for moments. 'Did she ask after me?'

'She's fine. A gal any father might be proud of. She ain't able to visit you, but she says you're welcome to go see her. I've given her fifty thousand pesos in silver which she plans to devote to her orphanage. She ain't a nun any more but she wants to go on doing good works. It's possible she might be gittin' hitched soon, too. A fine boy, a former priest.'

'Really?' Don Arturo frowned, as if surprised. 'That is good. She has my blessing.'

'Here's your share. Fifty thousand pesos. The rest goes to me as my fee.'

'He's cheating you.' Dona Andrea stepped out from behind the *haciendado*. 'He's keeping a hundred thousand pesos in coins and silver.'

'Waal, look who's here.' Slaughter rubbed his jaw and smiled. 'Fancy you crawling outa the woodwork.'

'You had better be careful what you say,' she hissed. 'You won't have the chance to humiliate me again.'

'Fifty thousand pesos was the agreed

reward,' Don Arturo said, in his quavering voice. 'Why do you want more?'

'OK, I'll settle for fifty thousand,' Slaughter drawled. 'But it's hid in the mountains. And so is the other fifty thousand in a different spot. You could say it's my insurance. You don't get directions on how to git your hands on it until I'm safe outa here and back in the United States. I'll write ya.'

'How can you believe him?' Andrea shrieked. 'He's not getting out of here until he tells us where it is. We'll make him talk. He's not so tough.' She clapped her hands. '*Hombres!* Show yourselves.'

Slaughter turned his horse and saw three villainous-looking desperadoes stroll out of the stable. Another appeared from the kitchen doorway. And two more rode in through the open gateway to block his escape. He glanced up at one of the turrets and saw a guard with a carbine in his hands show himself.

'So, you've gotten yourself a few more gallows birds?' He gave a scoffing grin as he faced Andrea again. She was dressed in her riding outfit, spurred boots, the leather split-skirt, a crisp white shirt, the stiff-brimmed hat, her face dark and hard, her hair pinned back. 'How's your ear?'

She darted her hand up to her missing earlobe and snarled, 'This time you won't get out of here alive.'

'So, Don Arturo, this is the way you pay me?' Slaughter drawled. 'I thought you were a gentleman. Did I hear you got married to this scorpion?'

'There was nothing I could do,' he quavered. 'I mean, I wanted to. We have been together a long time.'

'What you mean is, when I'd gone they brought in some cowardly priest and forced him to marry you. I bet you didn't have much say in the matter.'

He shook his head in a dazed way. No doubt they hadn't left any marks on his head to show the beating but there were probably plenty on his body, burns and blows and other tortures. 'You don't understand,' he faltered. 'Andrea deserves some reward.'

'Yeah, I see she's wearin' the pants.'

'Andrea,' Don Arturo said, raising his lofty head in the way he would have in the days when he expected to be obeyed. 'I promised this man his fifty thousand. Don't let's have trouble. I believe him when he says he will let us know where the rest is hidden. We have to have trust.'

'Rubbish!' she hissed. 'Get him, men.'

The gallows birds began to close in on him, one of them scraping a machete across his stubbled jaw. 'Ay, *gringo*. You wan' trouble, you come to right place.' The others' hands hovered over the guns in the holsters on their hips, confident they could take him.

Slaughter didn't hesitate. He hauled the mustang up on his back-hooves, gripped the Schofield and, arm extended, aimed at the one who could do most damage — 'Crash!' — he didn't wait to watch the gunman up in the tower somersault out onto the tiled roofs. He plunged his mustang forward scattering the three men coming out of the stable, twisting the horse around to take out the one firing from the kitchen doorway.

'Don't kill him yet!' he heard Dona Andrea scream. 'We need him alive.'

Good. That gave him a chance. But Slaughter felt bound by no such scruples with these scum. He whirled his mustang around in the dust of the courtyard and the Schofield crashed out again as he blasted one of the horsemen from his saddle. He took aim at the other rider but was scorched with pain as a bullwhip cracked by one of those on the ground curled around his neck. He grabbed at the rawhide whip with his left fist and jerked it from the man's hands.

But, at the same instant, the other's machete cut across his forearm, the shock searing through him, forcing him to drop the Schofield. Almost at the same moment he sensed a noose dropping over him and his shoulders were pinioned by a lariat. He was jerked from the saddle and hit the ground hard.

The wind knocked from him, Slaughter tried to clutch at the lariat as he was dragged away by the horseman, out of the gates, dragged pounding over rocks and scrub on a 'chicken ride'. He was hauled at a gallop back through the gates again, and pulled to his feet, covered in dust and blood to be pummelled by the remaining desperadoes. He doubled up and tensed himself against the blows.

'Right!' Dona Andrea shrieked. 'Put him over that wagon. He will soon tell us where the silver is hidden.'

'Go to hell,' Slaughter growled, struggling and kicking out at the men. 'You won't get nuthin' outa me.'

'Won't I?' She was standing before him, wielding the nine-foot bullwhip with its knotted tip. 'We'll soon see.'

He gasped as she slashed it across his

chest. He was roped, helplessly, back to the wagon and wondered, briefly, how long he could last as the whip whistled, cutting into his flesh again. What did the silver matter? No, he had to hold out. He saw Andrea smile, cruelly, as she tossed the whip away and took a knife from one of the grinning desperadoes.

'Hold his legs apart,' she ordered, stepping up close, staring into his eyes. 'I gave you the chance to have me,' she hissed, pricking the knife into his groin. 'But from now on you will never have any woman.'

'Damn you,' he gritted out. 'You bitch.'

Suddenly a pistol shot cracked out and the expression in Dona Andrea's eyes changed to fear and horror as she stumbled forward, clutching at Slaughter, sliding to the ground, the knife dropping from her hand, blood flowering on the back of her white shirt.

Slaughter saw the boy, Manolo, standing twenty paces away, gripping the Schofield in his hands, the barrel smoking. He must have run in and found it on the ground. He stood watching Andrea die. 'She tortured Don Arturo,' he stuttered out. 'She would have killed you.'

His mother, a woman called Candida, came running in from the *jacals*, clutching hold of her son, screaming when she saw the gun in his hands. 'What have you done?'

'I killed her,' the boy said. 'I had to.'

Slaughter eyed the desperadoes, one still on his horse. 'You had better cut me free and git outa here,' he snarled. 'Your boss woman is dead. You ain't gonna git nuthin' outa this.'

'*Si*, do as he says.' Don Arturo was standing in his doorway, a rifle in his hands, covering them. 'Get out of here, fast, and be thankful I let you go.'

The four low-lifes glanced at each other, then backed away to their horses, climbing into the saddles, kicking in their spurs and galloping from the courtyard away over the plain in a cloud of dust.

Manolo picked up the fallen knife and cut the Texan free. 'Who are you, mister?' he asked. 'What is your name?'

'Slaughter,' he said, looking around at the fallen. 'Kinda apt, ain't it?' He gave the boy a hug. 'Come on, kid. You did the right thing.'

Don Arturo had stepped across the courtyard and put an arm around Candida. 'You are the most honest and loving woman I know,' he said. 'Now our son has freed me I want you to do the honour of marrying me.'

Slaughter clutched at the blood streaming from his arm and staggered to lean against the wagon. 'Jeez,' he drawled, 'why didn't you do that years ago? It woulda saved us all this bother.' They were the last words he spoke before he slipped into unconsciousness.

★ ★ ★

Candida had tended his wounds and nursed him back to health. He had stayed for the wedding feast, and, although still feeling a tad weak from loss of blood, had saddled up his mustang and led Manolo to where he had stashed Don Arturo's silver.

'*Adios, amigo,*' he called, as he watched the boy ride away with the silver slung over his *burro*. 'Take care of your father.'

He loaded up his own share and headed towards the border, gradually descending from the mountains to the plain.

★ ★ ★

Juarez was a frontier town, named after Mexico's beneficent president, and full of the scum who haunt such places, smugglers of weapons and women, rustlers, murderers, petty thieves and mug-hunters, set on the south bank of the Rio Grande. Slaughter wandered in on his mustang from across a seemingly interminable plain of dreary thorn and rocks and needed to slake his thirst. He spotted a saloon named Flower of the

Desert, hitched his horse by a drinking trough, and ambled inside. He stood by the bar accustoming his eyes to the sudden shadows and glanced around through narrowed lids. At this early hour of the day there were just a few no-account idlers by the look of them.

He relaxed and drew off his torn gloves. 'Don't give me none of that *pulque*. You got any beer?'

'*Si, señor*.' A bottle of St Louis steam beer was produced. The barman twisted the cork and proudly presented it to him. '*Dos centavos*.'

Slaughter glugged it down his throat and gave a gasp of pleasure, wiping his mouth on the back of his hand. 'Gimme another. And I'll have some breakfast. *Heuvos rancheros*. OK?'

He sauntered over to a seat in a corner and propped his empty Winchester against the wall. He would be glad to get back to the States. These hot chilli *frijoles* were playing havoc with his guts. And the firewater didn't help. He chopped up the food and ate with his left hand, resting his right hand free on one knee as was his habit. A thin-faced peon standing at the bar kept looking shiftily his way. Slaughter scowled at him and he scurried off like a rat out of a hole. 'What's troubling him?' he muttered.

'Everything OK, *señor*?' The 'keep had come across, patted his shoulder and given him a wink. 'You like my wife?'

A fat, black-moustached lady of yellow complexion beamed at him from behind the bar, fluttering her pudgy fingers. 'Some flower,' he drawled. 'Nope, I'll pass. Jest cawfee'll do.'

Tonight, he thought, as he continued to munch through the pile of food, he would demolish a decent bottle of whiskey, or even, with any luck, a drop of the Rev. Bourbon's brew. And tomorrow he would start looking for a good piece of land.

The *peon*'s weasel face appeared over the batwing doors. 'There,' he hissed, pointing his way.

A tall American in sun-faded cavalry uniform pushed through. He wore boots, spurs, a forage cap, and a big Remington revolver stuck in his belt. He stood and stared intently at the dishevelled and scarred bounty hunter as another, slighter man, in frockcoat uniform and cockaded campaign hat, stepped in beside him, a similarly fierce look of disdain on his bearded face.

'Are you the man called Slaughter?' the tall officer, with braid knots denoting lieutenant on his sleeve, demanded in stentorian tones.

'What if I am?'

'We been looking for you a long time,' the more willowy one, who seemed to be some kind of captain, whispered, as his fingers unbuttoned the flap of the holster on his belt.

Slaughter forked some more black beans into his mouth and slowly chewed. 'You boys are interruptin' my breakfast. Is this official business?'

'No, it's a private matter,' the captain hissed. 'We got a score to settle with the man who gunned down Lieutenant Sandy Melchor. He was by way of bein' a friend of ourn.'

'That was a long time ago.' Slaughter poked at his food with the fork. 'Take my advice, boys, let it rest.'

'You lousy, stinkin' coward,' the big man shouted. 'You shot him in the back. You shoulda been strung up.'

Slaughter ceased eating, his fork poised, his green eyes flickering as he took a glance their way. 'In that case it can't be me. I never shot a man down without letting him go for his gun. And, if possible, I prefer to warn a fella, like I'm warnin' you two: go away, and forget this.'

'We don't fergit.' The smaller one stepped a pace or two away from his friend. 'In our company we're men of the feud. Where do you want it, you filthy Johnny Reb — in here, or outside?'

'Come on, woman-killer,' the big man boomed, his hand snaking towards the butt of the Remington. 'Stand up

241

and take your medicine.'

'She was my wife fer Chris' sakes. He was in bed with her. What was I expected to do?' Slaughter gave a scream of agony, his free right hand bringing out the Schofield from its greased holster. He was turning, fanning the hammer, crashing out shots, first at the big lieutenant, whose own bullet went wild, smashing the plate from the table, and, secondly, at the captain whose draw was hindered by his holster flap. Both men stared at him with momentary horror, and toppled to the floor like felled trees.

'It's gettin' like a man cain't have a quiet meal any more.' Slaughter rose to his feet, blowing down the barrel of his smoking gun. 'I don't like killin' so-called officers and gentlemen but they forced my hand, you saw that. Remember to tell whoever asks.' He looked down at the two foolish corpses, made the sign of the cross and drawled, 'Rest in peace, boys.'

He flipped a silver peso to the

barman, took his Winchester and strolled to the door. '*Adios*.'

He ambled his horse slowly through the town as people, aroused by the shooting, watched him go. He crossed the dirty old Rio Grande and climbed towards El Paso. 'Maybe I can get some peace now,' he muttered to himself. He knew his war with the world was over. But he also knew that in the wilds of New Mexico, where he was headed, there were too many killers about — both redmen and whitemen — to whom peace was an alien word.

He stepped down outside the saloon in which he had first met Manolo, the boy who had given him the torn half-page of the Bible. 'Hi,' the owner greeted him. 'Where you been to?'

'Hell an' back, sortin' out a few thangs.' His face split into a grin as he spotted a bottle on a shelf. 'Gimme a glass of that bourbon. An' make it a big one. I got me a thirst.'

Other titles in the
Linford Western Library:

SMOKING STAR

B. J. Holmes

In the one-horse town of Medicine Bluff two men were dead. Sheriff Jack Starr didn't need the badge on his chest to spur him into tracking the killer. He had his own reason for seeking justice, a reason no-one knew. It drove him to take a journey into the past where he was to discover something else that was to add even greater urgency to the situation — to stop Montana's rivers running red with blood.

THE WIND WAGON

Troy Howard

Sheriff Al Corning was as tough as they came and with his four seasoned deputies he kept the peace in Laramie — at least until the squatters came. To fend off starvation, the settlers took some cattle off the cowmen, including Jonas Lefler. A hard, unforgiving man, Lefler retaliated with lynchings. Things got worse when one of the squatters revealed he was a former Texas lawman — and no mean shooter. Could Sheriff Corning prevent further bloodshed?

RIVERBOAT

Alan C. Porter

When Rufus Blake died he was found to be carrying a gold bar from a Confederate gold shipment that had disappeared twenty years before. This inspires Wes Hardiman and Ben Travis to swap horse and trail for a riverboat, the *River Queen*, on the Mississippi, in an effort to find the missing gold. Cord Duval is set on destroying the *River Queen* and he has the power and the gunmen to do it. Guns blaze as Hardiman and Travis attempt to unravel the mystery and stay alive.

McKINNEY'S LAW

Mike Stotter

McKinney didn't count on coming across a dead body in the middle of Texas. He was about to become involved in an ever-deepening mystery. The renegade Comanche warrior, Black Eagle, was on the loose, creating havoc; he didn't appear in McKinney's plans at all, not until the Comanche forced himself into his life. The US Army gave McKinney some relief to his problems, but it also added to them, and with two old friends McKinney set about bringing justice through his own law.

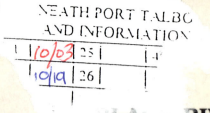
BLACK RIVER

Adam Wright

John Dyer has come to the insignificant little town of Black River to destroy the last living reminder of his dark past. He has come to kill. Jack Hart is determined to stop him. Only he knows the terrible truth that has driven Dyer here, and he knows that only he can beat Dyer in a gunfight. Ex-lawman Brad Harris is after Dyer too — to avenge his family. The stage is set for madness, death and vengeance.